COUP DE GRASS

A bit of competition for Detective Sergeant Boggis? A strange policeman cutting himself in on Peeper the snout's services? All is possible in the shadowy world of crime. When he tried to serve two masters, Peeper found himself on the proverbial slippery slope. Should he go for the young, brash newcomer or the trusty old stager? The young bloke might last longer. On the other hand, whilst he might be miserable, cantankerous and tight-fisted, Bert Boggis wasn't a bad old swine at heart.

PADDER NASH

COUP
DE GRASS

Complete and Unabridged

LINFORD
Leicester

First published in Great Britain

First Linford Edition
published 1996

British Library CIP Data

Nash, Padder
    Coup de grass.—Large print ed.—
Linford mystery library
I. Title II. Series
823.914 [F]

ISBN 0–7089–7854–1

Published by
F. A. Thorpe (Publishing) Ltd.
Anstey, Leicestershire

Set by Words & Graphics Ltd.
Anstey, Leicestershire
Printed and bound in Great Britain by
T. J. Press (Padstow) Ltd., Padstow, Cornwall

This book is printed on acid-free paper

1

HALF the trouble with the Golden Roof Restaurant is the shocking low class of person you meet there. The other half is a composite of the muck they sell in solid and liquid form and the widespread smell and untidiness of the place itself. Vince Skinner, the proprietor, falls four square into both categories, except that he's round and he can't fall. Vince is as low as they come — so low that he'd be flat on his face if he wasn't too fat to lie down. Rumour has it that he actually eats his own pies and sausage rolls — grabs snacks throughout the day — which, if true, explains why he's a twenty stone Humpty Dumpty with an antisocial nature. You can smell Vince coming — and to complete the picture, he makes the place look untidy.

But Vince Skinner wasn't bothering

me much on the day I speak of. Nothing much was bothering me at all. For once in a rare while, Skinner's Caff (the same Golden Roof Restaurant) was a tolerable setting in which to consume standard quality gnat's-pee tea. The three prostitutes round a table in the far corner were chattering quietly and not ripping each other's throats out, and the only other customer apart from me — a grey-haired old chap, not of these parts, who was nibbling a spud tart and looking bewildered — didn't look strong enough to bother anybody. If you happened to glance upwards, something I frequently do in Skinner's Caff, you could see one or two smears of ancient gold paint on the ceiling, proving that the customary pall of acrid smoke had almost dispersed. I have a rooted objection to breathing other people's cast-off smoke, so I was more than pleased, and the fact that I happened to be sucking away at a small cigar was neither here nor there.

No man has a right to be that

complacent and I should have known better. I was happily puffing, slurping and watching the passing scene through Vince's manky windows when a couple of motor cyclists roared up and parked their nasty, noisy machines on the pavement. I've learned to live with motor bikes. They make people deaf, poison the atmosphere and deprave and corrupt the people who ride them. On top of that, they kill people — and they're made in Japan, which is the greatest of all their faults. But like I say, I've learned to live with them — and I can even live with the louts and yobboes who burn them through the streets. Oh hell! I don't mean *all* motor cyclists. I'm just talking about the ones who hang about the Golden Roof Restaurant. They're all one sort — all hard and swaggering — and I get along with them fairly well. But I wish they'd take those brown fish tanks off their heads occasionally.

These two stalked into Skinner's Caff looking like stand-ins for Buzz Aldrin.

They breasted the counter, still wearing full regalia as though they could only breathe with their boxes on — a view I had some sympathy with. I watched Skinner doing his stuff with the teapot, then I lost interest and went back to goggling out of the window. But in less than half a minute my interest perked up again, because one of the plastic robots minced over and sat down at the table, right next to me.

"Hiya, Peeper," he said.

I'm able to tell you exactly what he said, even though his voice was muffled, but I didn't have a clue who he was. I decided to let it lie a bit though, because sometimes it's manners not to ask. So I just let him have a 'Hello' back and grinned as though he was my truest and dearest friend.

"I got a job for you to do," he said.

Now that made things a bit different. My status in the work stakes is *unemployed*, and has been for a lot of years. I do turn my hand to gain — and regularly — but the field of my operations is strictly limited — particularly the range of people I work for — and whoever this spectacle in brass, perspex and leather might be, he wasn't anybody I contracted with. So I was on my guard in a loose sort of way. Suspicious, but not ready to turn and flee.

"I ain't looking for a job," I informed the man.

"You'll like this one."

"Who says so?"

"I do. This one's right up your street, Peeper."

I don't like people calling me *Peeper*, especially when I can't look them in the face, but it's been going on for so long now that I've stopped grumbling. Except to Bert Boggis, that is. Bert was the one who started it, so I make a point of always grumbling to him.

"Somebody recommended me, did they?" I asked him.

5

"I recommended you myself. You're a natural for it, and I should know. I've seen your stuff, Peeper."

This was getting to be quite a puzzle. The line he was feeding me had a ring of truth to it, but it was a home truth, and a bit too close for comfort. In my profession it pays to be unobtrusive in your doings. I'd always been ultra-careful. I couldn't imagine how this tin-pot street bandit could have seen my stuff. I couldn't even imagine how he could possibly know I had any stuff, what it was like or how I put it to use. By all the laws, he couldn't know a blind thing about me — unless . . . I stared hard at the big roll of brown plastic where his face ought to be and wondered a hell of a lot.

"You got the advantage of me," I told him. "You seem to know me, but I sure as hell don't know you. Where did we meet, friend?"

"You work for Detective Sergeant Boggis," he said.

6

Do I, now? And if I do, how the hell have you cottoned on? Don't tell me Boggis has been sounding off again? I thought the questions but I didn't ask them — and I didn't blurt out any admissions either. I just stared straight back at the bloke and hoped my look said what it was supposed to say — that he was blind bonkers.

"Detective Sergeant who?"

"Boggis. Bert Boggis. The local chap."

"Never heard of him," I told him firmly. "Boggis, you say? Come off it, chum. Nobody on earth has a name like Boggis."

"Now you're messing me around," the bloke said, with a sharp edge to his voice, "and I wouldn't do that if I were you. I don't like clever buggers. I like to be friendly."

Maybe he did, but he didn't sound in the least friendly. He sounded a lot too tough for my liking and I've met some of the toughest over the years. But I wasn't being brow-beaten.

I squared my shoulders and sneered in his face.

"I pick my friends, chum, and as far as I know you're not one of 'em. Nor is this Bogshite bloke you mentioned. So if you don't mind, I'd like to finish my tea in peace."

He didn't make a move to leave, but some of the bluster went out of him and for all I know he might even have grinned.

"You know Bert Boggis. You're his snout."

"His snout? What is he then, a pig?"

"Now you're making jokes, Peeper. But you're only wasting time. I'm a pig too, if you want to put it that way. Detective Constable Warburton. You met me a while back."

"You got the wrong number, chum. It was some other bloke."

"The Bragg-Norton job, Peeper. You remember the Bragg-Norton job."

Now memory is a very funny thing. Sometimes you have it and sometimes

8

not. If you have it, you might want to mention it, or then again you might not. I wasn't sure what the hell I wanted. But I remembered the Bragg-Norton job all right.

2

A JUNE day. Soft, balmy weather. I leaned back on the park bench to enjoy it. The ducks quacked at me like old friends and waddled their backsides in salute. The milk grey water of the pond rose to shade itself in long dark ripples, the breeze sighed in the bushes, the sun played shadow painting with scuts of drifting cloud and all was peace in Gresham Park.

There was a big lump of silence after Boggis joined me on the bench. I could have broken it, but I wouldn't. I can be as bloody-minded as he can. Bert Boggis likes to pass himself off as the strong, silent type. In special cases — and I'm one — he likes to show how independent he can be, and one of his ploys is to act as though he admits of nothing outside the circle of his skull. He was using it now. When he

10

was satisfied that I'd taken the point, he looked up and grunted.

"Make it rapid, Peeper. I'm a busy man."

"You want speed?" I said. "All right then, don't go irritating me the way you do. Damn it to hell, Bert, can't you call me something else but *Peeper*?"

"Sure, if you like. But I don't like using cuss-words."

"You can't even be bloody polite," I told him.

"Listen, Peeper. I've no time to prattle about silly things like that. You should change your name if it bothers you. Go on, then. What would you like me to call you?"

"Skip it," I said sullenly. I knew I was flogging a dead horse. I'd flogged it for years and it had been dead all the time. But being called *Peeper* is like having false teeth — I can never get to like it. I know what a peeper is, you see, and I'm quite definitely not one. Boggis knows my feelings on the subject — he's heard them often enough — but he keeps calling me *Peeper* out of spite. He looked at me now, nearly deadpan but with just a slight twist to his mouth and the suspicion of a twitch on his cheek. He was laughing at me. He was having his little bit of fun at my expense and the less I liked it the better the fun.

"Take that smirk off your chops," I told him.

"Come on Peeper. Stop arsing around. You sent a little bird to chirp in my ear — so what's in the offing?"

I took a small package from my jacket pocket, laid it on the bench between us and turned back the hessian cover to show him the item. It lay there like a lump of goats' milk cheese, waiting to be sliced in half and fed to us for picnic lunch, but I didn't have a knife sharp enough or an arm strong enough to cut it, and I sure as hell wouldn't have enjoyed the taste. And yet, in a sense, the stuff looked good enough to eat. It had the shape of a jumbo chocolate bar, a thick oblong base tapering to upper slopes like a very shallow and elongated pyramid, and its flat upper surface had a runny, creamy gleam. There was quite a slice of it. As chocolate it would have cost you a bob or two, but as anybody could tell at a glance, it was worth a hell of a lot more.

"You know what that stuff is, Peeper?" Boggis said, as he got ready to air his own knowledge.

"Silver," I said.

"You got any idea where it's from?" He went on. He was evidently most disappointed that I'd cleared the first hurdle.

"Bragg-Norton Chrome Company."

More disappointment for Boggis. He badly wanted to tell me something I didn't already know, but he wasn't having much joy. Still, he had the guts to make one more effort.

"And you know where the Bragg-Norton place is?"

"Long Canton Trading Estate, over at Mortley."

"That's bang on the nail, clever sod," he said sadly, "and in case you hadn't thought about it, that's right off my patch."

I looked at Boggis with new-found respect. At last he'd come up with something I'd never even considered. It isn't surprising really. As a member of the Great British Public you tend not to think about such things, but I suppose if you happen to be a copper you have to bear it in mind.

"It's only just down the road," I pointed out.

"Exactly." He flashed me a queer look. "And what a pity it isn't up the road, or even across the road. But it's down the road, Peeper, and that puts it in an entirely different police force area."

* * *

A buggeration factor in an otherwise straightforward little job. It hadn't seemed like much at the time, but

14

in the long run it had laid me open to a whole bagful of risks. And this leather-jacketed speed freak sitting in front of me now was bidding to be yet another risk. If the bloke really was who he claimed to be — and I was damned near sure of it — he was a copper from that different police force area that Boggis had spoken of. There had been a Warburton, I remembered, and this sounded like him. All I needed for a clincher was a look at his face.

"Don't you ever get hot and sweaty under those things?" I asked him.

"Some. You get used to it. But don't change the subject, Peeper. I'm here to strike a deal."

"What sort of deal?"

"One that'll bring you a nice profit if it comes off."

"And suppose it doesn't come off? I do time — is that it?"

His helmet rocked a bit from side to side and moved a few inches in my direction. I supposed he was giving me a shrewd look.

"There's always that, Peeper," he said, "but you know how it goes. We're both in the risk business, one way and another."

"Speak for yourself," I told him. "I'm an out-of-work labourer and I haven't the slightest notion who you are. I'm not even sure I should be talking to you. You could be a Russian spy."

"I've told you, I'm a police officer."

"Name of Warburton — that's what you said."

"That's right."

"And you want to talk to me about some job?"

"I could use a good informant. I've got a thing going."

I stopped a while to have another long think. This lad was either stupid or naïve. If he imagined for a minute he could strike up a profitable working arrangement on the strength of a quick chat-up in a mucky caff he was short on research. But from what he'd told me so far, that was what he had in mind. I wondered what my mate Bert Boggis would think about this — if I decided to tell him. And from that thought I moved on naturally to wondering whether I should tell Boggis. But this was early days and the barter hadn't started yet. I asked myself what this young Warburton might be worth in terms of rake-off — a couple of quid would probably be his mark, I reckoned. And I wasn't in the market for chicken feed, not after the tidy sum I'd just collected for the Bragg-Norton job.

"O.K. Chum," I said. "Let's give you credit for being half right. Let's pretend I do know this Bogwell fellow you mentioned, and just for a minute let's kid each other that I'd ever have truck with cops. I don't do business with petrol pumps. Why don't you lift that lamp-shade off your nut and let me see your face?"

Warburton seemed reluctant, but he did as he was told. Minus the hat he looked less intimidating. His face was pink and sweaty and his hair was plastered down over his ears, but I recognized him, no trouble. The last time I'd clapped eyes on this face had been at Mortley, when I'd been crouched in the back seat of Bert Boggis's old banger of a Consul — and Warburton had been sitting in a bus shelter, chatting to Billy Miles.

* * *

And Mortley, that town next door, was outside Bert's bailiwick. Sitting on that bench in Gresham Park, Boggis himself had told me so.

I looked at Boggis for signs that he was kidding and decided he wasn't. But with Boggis you can never be completely sure. He has more colours of mood than a set of strobe lights and changes them just as often. If he'd changed his suit with the same frequency, maybe he'd have come up, now and then, with something that fitted him.

You know what I mean by a snazzy dresser? Bert Boggis isn't. I've often thought the rumours must be true, that he has a contract with the local mortuary assistant to buy up dead men's clothes cheap. Very often the colour's O.K. and the cloth top quality, but when you've said that, you've said it all. Like that day, for example. He had on a pair of black pin-stripe pants originally made for a podgy lawyer with ducks' disease — and in case I haven't said so already, Bert Boggis is a tall, scrawny bloke with pins like a pair of chopsticks. I watched him cross his legs and pull the pant-cuffs down over his knees like a nervous tart playing with her skirt. Which didn't help his jacket, plain black, made for a lawyer as well, I should imagine, but a thinner lawyer altogether. That was stretched tight across Bert's shoulders and looked set to split wide open if he coughed.

My God! And I'm shackled to you for life, I said to myself. And I meant it, every word. Detective Sergeant

Albert Boggis is just about the most undesirable acquaintance you could possibly dream up. I don't only mean undesirable to me, I mean undesirable to anybody with a pinch of common sense. He doesn't have any of the basic qualities you'd look for in a mate. I regard as some of the great mysteries of life the facts that Bert Boggis has a wife, (a cracking piece of stuff and a very friendly person) who seems to love him, or at any rate goes on living with him in apparent tranquillity; has a couple of kids who fondly believe they have a decent type as a father and has bosses who must at one time have thought he was an all-right bloke — else why the hell would they have promoted him to sergeant? Heaven help me, I still like him a bit myself. I used to like him quite a lot, but that was before I found out what a bitter and twisted sod he can be.

I'm not just being bitchy, by the way. He really is a twit of the highest order, yet for more years than I care to remember he's been a close associate of mine. In a manner of speaking, I feed him. I offer him food, that is, and he eats it every time. But he only picks up the bill if he happens to like the fare, and I have to accept his judgment. No waiter would make a deal like that, or keep it running for nigh on twenty years, but then I'm not a waiter, and I have to be committed to one customer.

"So it's out of your area," I said, after a moment musing. "Is that bad, Bert?"

"It isn't good, Peeper. It makes life difficult."

"You mean you can't use this at all?"

"Not very well. It isn't my crime, you see."

"Can't you sort of act proxy?" I suggested.

"Well, yes and no. I can take that ingot and see it gets back to the right people, but I can't guarantee more than a few quid for you — a hand-out from the poor box."

21

"A few quid, eh? Right ho, Bert. The deal's off."

Quick as a flash I gathered the lump of loot into its hessian wrapping, got up and walked away, stuffing the bundle into my jacket pocket as I went. Bert Boggis doesn't often move fast, but he did this time. He was right behind me in a trice, his fingers scrabbling at my collar and his hot breath in my earhole.

"Come back you silly nit. You can't just walk away like that."

"Who's going to stop me?" I wanted to know.

"I am. What you've got there is stolen property."

"That's what I thought," I said, relenting. "And since you're a cop, I should have thought you'd be glad to take it off my hands. But don't give it another thought, Bert. If you don't want it, I can quite easily find somebody else who does."

"You forget your place, Peeper," Boggis said sternly. "You could do

22

time for that little bitty ingot you're carrying. You know it's hot and so do I. And I've caught you red-handed, so what's to stop me huffing you, right now, and charging you with theft?"

"You officious swine. You wouldn't dare."

"Don't dare me, chum, or you might get a big surprise. Now start showing a bit of sense, man. Park your backside on that bench and we'll think of ways of tackling this latest damned fiasco of yours."

I sashayed back to the bench and sat down, wary as a mouse.

"I'm not playing for just a few quid, Bert. You must be bonkers. That's a fair old lump. Best part of a hundred quid's worth."

"You're not often right, Peeper, and you're wrong again. It's worth double that. Two hundred of anybody's money."

"What's that? An inspired guess?"

"I'm not guessing, old lad. That's exactly what it's worth."

"Well, Bert Boggis, you old clever clogs. How the hell did you work that out? I only showed you this bit of treasure five minutes ago, and you've never so much as touched it, never mind hefted it."

"No need. I saw a crime message about it, just this morning."

"You crafty sod. You already knew it was missing, didn't you."

"But of course. I never miss a trick, Peeper. You ought to know that by now. And if you'll permit me, I'll give you another detail that has escaped you. That lump of silver wasn't on its own. Whoever the team was that ripped off the Bragg-Norton place, they did a proper job. They shifted forty ingots and got 'em clean away."

"Good Heavens, Bert. You mean we can multiply this by forty?"

"That's what I'm telling you. And one little ingot's no use to me, Peeper. I want the other thirty-nine as well. I want the lot."

I grinned at him, and I kept the

look frozen on my face till I could see he was itching to know *why* I was grinning. It isn't often I can score over Bert Boggis, but this time I thought I'd managed it.

"You've got it wrong, Bert. Not once, but three times."

"How do you make that out?"

"It's a question of numbers mainly. They didn't nick forty, they nicked fifty. And anyway, it wasn't a they — it was only a him."

"That's good. It makes the job a lot easier. Who is he?"

"Never mind who. I might tell you later, or I might not."

"Don't mess me around, Peeper. I want his name — right now."

"And then there's the third thing, Bert," I went on, ignoring his outburst. "He nicked the silver, but he didn't shift it away."

"Cut out the conundrums. What are you trying to tell me?"

"The stuff's still there, Bert. Hidden away somewhere in the factory. He

25

brought a sample out to show to a buyer and he won't shift the rest of the stuff till he's hammered out a price."

★ ★ ★

After that, I told Boggis the story — and now I'll tell it to you.

The Master Mind behind the Bragg-Norton silver ingots job was the same Billy Miles I mentioned earlier and he was working strictly on his own. I can safely tell you his name, because he's working for the Queen now, and will be for the next five years. And although I know a hell of a lot about him, he knows damn all about me. He doesn't know who I am, what I look like or how I was able to hand him over to Bert Boggis on a plate.

Miles blundered into my life by accident, when he booked a room at the Albion Hotel and came under the influence of my good friend Stella. If you picture the Artful Dodger and add ten years, imagine Quasimodo and remove the hump, think about Sweeney Todd minus his razor, mix them all together and stir in a few choice bits of Cinderella's ugly sisters you've got a fair idea of Billy Miles, his appearance and his morals. No self-respecting proprietor of any proper hotel would have given him sanctuary, even in the coal shed, but the Albion Hotel is the sort of place where anybody can stay, and Stella, well, she's not to be compared with the self-respecting proprietor of any place.

Mind you, I mustn't be too unkind to Stella. She's a hell of a nice person really, and she runs her little business with all the style and efficiency of a stray whippet in charge of dustbins at the Council tip. People like Billy Miles are the salt of the earth to Stella. She welcomes them with open arms, takes a personal interest in their welfare, feeds them like fighting cocks and does her level best to turn them into decent citizens. She collects down-and-outs, scavengers, inadequates, parasites and ruffians of all kinds and packs them into her place for all the world as though she was working for the Sally Army. Why does she do it? It can only be out of the kindness of her heart. It isn't for the money, that's for sure, because seven out of ten of them pay a week's bed and board about once a month and the others never pay at all. I've spent years trying to figure out how she can afford to do it, and I'm still no wiser. Either she hit the pools for top weight some time, stashed the loot and kept her mouth shut, or she's got a rich uncle somewhere who's a bank manager.

For a long time, Bert Boggis suspected her of being a high-class fence, but that isn't the explanation either. Not that the opportunity doesn't exist. Hell, it's there every day of the week. Honest lodgers at the Albion can be counted on the fingers of one foot. A few of her guests are retired now, in the sense that they're too old to do anything except hobble about and wait to die, but half the others are out most nights, mugging Old Age Pensioners, screwing houses or raping women, and the other half are out most days, bouncing bad cheques, flogging worthless shares under false names or shoplifting. Highly dubious produce flows in and out of the Albion Hotel like sprats at a fish quay and I'm terrified of peeking into some of the rooms in case I stumble on illicit stills, banknote forging gear or flowering cannabis plants.

But you can be quite sure of one thing; Stella takes no rake-off whatever from any of this merchandise. She plays holy hell with anybody she catches with knock-off gear, and after they've had the length of her tongue she pleads with them to mend their ways and never gives up till they've promised to restore the stuff to its rightful owner. They seldom do, of course, but the cameras or colour tellies or cartons of fags get spirited away, leaving Stella with a clear conscience.

If she's as honest as I say, why

doesn't she turn all these crooks over to the cops? There are two very good reasons. In the first place, Stella loves people and can't stand making trouble for them. In the second, she hates cops with a deep and bitter hatred — a hatred so deep and bitter that even I, her dearest friend, have more than once been driven to wonder whence it sprang, and what dreadful confrontations she might have suffered in her dark and secret past. And if you think I've just contradicted myself, let me put you right. In Stella's eyes, people and cops are two vastly different things, which explains why she'd never dream of shopping one to the other.

Don't fret, though. The dark-hearted and light-fingered residents of the Albion Hotel don't always get away scot free. That's where I come in. I have a firm agreement with Bert Boggis that he'll give the place a wide berth — he's shit scared of Stella, anyway — and he leaves it to me to filter out little details of mutual interest and profit. For my part, I make damned sure that nobody ever gets lifted till he's well clear of Stella's place. Stella would be a mite put-out — hell no, she'd be flaming mad — if she ever found out how much of her pillow talk gets back, through me, to Boggis. That's the only thing in the whole world that ever sends a twinge of conscience. I don't give a damn about rogues, but I feel a bit of a bastard for using Stella the way I do.

But I do — and that brings me right back to Billy Miles. I noticed Billy hanging about the place and I knew he'd booked in, but apart from wondering how anybody could look so damned unpleasant all the time, I thought little about him. It was Stella who gave him a shove my way, and Stella who tipped me off about the silver.

We'd spent an hour in her boudoir and, as usual, she was lashing up the grub in the kitchen. This is Stella's way, and I'm all for it. You use energy, she says, so you replace it. That means bacon butties invariably follow bed.

I was standing there, with fat running down my chin, when I clapped eyes on the little hessian bundle. I prodded it open. Now I'm not an expert in bullion, but I've nicked a hundredweight or two of lead in my time and I knew it wasn't lead. In fact, I could have christened it straight off, because I'm good at bursts of intuition, but I thought I'd let Stella enlighten me.

"What the hell is that?" I squeaked.

"It's a lump of metal of some sort."

"Blast it, woman, I can see that. Where did you get it?"

"I was cleaning his room. I found it under the bed."

"Give me a break, Stella. Whose room?"

"That nice Mr. Miles. The new lodger."

I looked at her a bit old-fashioned. I wouldn't have said he was nice, and looking back on things I can tell you he's anything but, only I didn't know the bloke then, so I made allowances.

"Oh hell. You're at it again, aren't you. It's no business of yours, Stella. Why the hell didn't you leave it where it was?"

"Oh no. I think it's valuable. I'm going to talk to him about it. The poor man might be in some sort of trouble."

And I let the conversation drop at that stage. Why? Because I didn't have to ask what was in Stella's mind. Poor old Billy Miles was in for a rough time when he came round to collect his belongings, as he surely would. The old *help that lame dog over the stile* instinct was working overtime again and the hot hand of redemption — not to mention the clucking tongue — was due to be given full flow at the first opportunity. To be utterly honest, I had another reason for holding off. You don't come by lumps of valuable metal all that often and I badly wanted to know where Miles had acquired his. There might be a percentage in it for me, somewhere along the line, and one of my life-long golden rules is that when something starts to interest me I pretend not to give a damn. So I eased back nice and gently from the brink of the abyss.

"Suit yourself," I told her. "But if you've got a gab session coming with Billy Miles I want no part of it. I'd better skedaddle."

"There's no hurry," she said, all innocence. "He works you know. Some place over at Mortley. He doesn't get home till six."

★ ★ ★

So I hung about for an hour or so, talking about other things, and then I gave her a *cheerio* and left. It helps if I explain that I don't live at the Albion Hotel. I've got another set-up elsewhere, nice and cosy, with a girl called Doreen. I'll tell you about it some time. But I drop in on Stella most days and she doesn't seem to find anything odd in my comings and

34

goings. And I'll add to that — because it turns out to be relevant — that I hardly ever visit Stella twice in the same day. If that ever happens, it's because I have a hell of a good reason. I had the reason. It was going to happen today.

So I mooned about town for the rest of the day, had lunch with Doreen, went for a few pints of bitter and finished up practising pots at the billiard hall. But my heart wasn't in any of it. I kept checking my watch and shaking the damned thing to make sure it wasn't running in reverse, and all the time there was a little image bobbing about in my mind like a bluebottle on a bedroom window. Only it wasn't a bluebottle. It wasn't even blue. Hell, no. It was brick-shaped and rich looking, with a lovely, shiny, silvery cast.

By five to six I was back at the Albion Hotel, or to be more precise I was holed up in a bus shelter across the street. I saw Billy Miles drop off a bus. He was wearing overalls and carrying a canvas tommy-bag draped on a shoulder strap. He went straight past me without a glance — hadn't a clue who I was — and I watched him nip up the steps and disappear inside the Albion. My timing after that was an essay in perfection, but let me admit straight off, it was no miracle. I knew Stella, you see. She was on a rampage of do-good fervour and she was bound to be just as impatient as me, so there was no way Billy Miles could get past the threshold and up the stairs without clashing with her. The wash and brush up bit and the change of clothes would have to wait. The tough little finger would tap him on the shoulder, and while she wouldn't exactly frog-march him through to the kitchen, to the kitchen he would surely go. By the time I went in myself, no more than thirty seconds behind him, they were far too involved with each other to pay any attention to me.

You can be sure I know my way

round that hotel. There are various useful places and over the years I've made it my business to learn about them. Stella's kitchen — the arena for nearly all her contrived confrontations — is at the back of the building, reached by a corridor, and there's a certain stronghold quality about it. The guests seldom go there unless summoned, and they can't get near the kitchen by accident, because the corridor doesn't lead anywhere else. But if you nip through the dining-room, past the 'Ladies' toilet and through a door marked 'Private. No Admittance', you come to a long narrow room that's hardly ever used. In the old days before Stella took the place over, it was the family dining-room, and where would you expect the family dining-room to be, except right next to the kitchen? The connecting-door is still there. Stella always keeps it locked, but by chance it's a shockingly badly fitted door, great gaps at the bottom and down one side, and if you bung your ear against the nearest crack you can hear what's going on inside, just as if you were in the room.

They were already talking when I took up station, but it was just preliminary fencing and I waited for things to develop. What I heard over the next twenty minutes or so was absolute vintage Stella. She really is good, that woman. She could talk a flasher into stitching up his flies. It's a great pity she hates coppers so much, because she'd have made a good 'un, and once she'd graduated to C.I.D. — a foregone conclusion — she'd have made the rough, tough professionals like Bert Boggis look like amateurs. Since I'm no stranger to the interrogation business myself, I'll allow that she starts with two massive advantages. She's a woman and can make good use of women's tricks. And she lets it be known, with convincing honesty, that her victims have nothing to fear. Billy Miles had nothing to fear from her, but he had from me, and I hoped to God that neither he nor Stella would ever find out.

Miles started off with bluster, denied all knowledge of the ingot and threatened her with a beating and a lawsuit in that order. But he was putty in her hands. In no time at all, he'd pulled his horns in and started to offer her a partnership in the proceeds. She wouldn't have that, of course, but she played it for a while before chopping it off. After that, his voice started to sound husky and he told her all about his previous convictions and how he'd be locked up till the bars rusted if the cops caught him. He offered to be a good boy in future and pleaded with her not to chuck him out on his ear. Stella assured him that he was all right at the Albion for life, so long as he mended his wicked ways. Then the kettle went on and the eggs and bacon started sizzling in the big pan, and all the time she was preparing the feast she was feeding him good, sound sense as she saw it. I tell you, I'm bloody grateful she never comes that line with me, or I'd just have to tell her a lot of things I sure as hell don't want her to know.

While I listened, Billy Miles spilled his innermost secrets till I knew everything about him, except maybe the colour of his underpants, and he'd have told her about that, too, if she hadn't been a lady. He told her all about his job at the Bragg-Norton factory, how he'd found his way to the silver, how much of it he'd managed to nick and where he'd planted the rest of the ingots ready for later collection. When he told her he'd pulled the job alone and unaided I was cynical enough to think he might be telling fibs, but I put myself right on that point. The way Stella was working on him, and the way he was responding to her, he had to be telling the truth.

It will be enough if I summarize the rest of the stuff I picked up. He'd been sounding out the market and he was expecting a phone call from Dominic Hassall. I know Hassall very well. He's a bent bullion dealer. Billy had only told Hassall about the one ingot and he was holding back on the rest till he could size up the offer.

Stella wasn't over the moon with the Hassall angle. She wanted Billy Miles to take the ingot back and smuggle it into the factory, then fob Hassall off with some old story when he rang. But Miles stuck out a bit on that one — and in the end, they compromised.

"He knows about it now — so I got to flog it to him," Miles said.

"Well, all right, Billy. But just the one. I think I can let you off for just one, so long as you don't tell him about the others."

"But damn it all, Stella, I got a fortune tucked away down at the factory. What the hell am I supposed to do with it?"

"Let it lie and save your soul."

"All right, Stella. If that's what you want, I'll do it."

I'll swear he didn't say it grudgingly or in bad grace. He seemed content to settle for small mercies. But right after that he must have made a move to pick up the ingot and spirit it away into his pocket, because I heard Stella say — in a very snappy way:

"Oh no, Billy. That stays where it is. You can pick it up later when the man calls. I want to be there, to stop you making a fool of yourself."

★ ★ ★

I slipped away at that stage and my immediate plan was to go haring off to a phone box and pass the word to Boggis. I moved with caution, because I didn't want Stella to know I'd visited her twice in one day, even though my reasons had been good, strong ones. Somehow, I felt she wouldn't have understood — or maybe she would, which would have been a damned sight worse.

But as chance would have it, I got held up. It was one of those mad spins of luck that you sometimes get, and it fitted the last piece in place for me. As I was tip-toeing through the lobby I heard the reception desk phone put out that queer initial gurgle and before it could give a full-blooded ring I had the handset off its cradle. It was a moment for decision, and I decided I had to take a chance. So I stood with the phone in my hand while I looked along the far corridor towards the kitchen door. It was still tight shut. It had to be, I realized, because although Stella and Billy Miles had bottomed out their main topic and thrashed it near to death, there was still the matter of the fry-up she was serving him, and it would take him at least a minute or two to wolf it down. I didn't think they could possibly have heard the phone ring, or Stella would have been out before now to snatch at the chance of a customer. While I was thinking all this, I had time to decide not to be myself, and it's as well I did, because when I asked the phone, in an uncharacteristic croak, whom I had the honour of addressing, it turned out to be Dominic Hassall himself, and Hassall would more than likely have recognized my real voice.

"Can I be of any service?" I enquired hoarsely.

"You can fetch Billy Miles to the phone."

"Sorry, I can't do that. Mr. Miles isn't home yet. He must have been delayed." These were pure delaying tactics and I was making them up as I went along.

"Bastard." Hassall said, flouting the Telephone Company bye-laws. "The bloody man said he'd be in tonight."

"Can I get him to ring you back?"

"No. I got better things to do with my time. But you can tell him I rang. And tell him this, too. I'll ring again tomorrow night, same time, and the bugger better be there."

"Very well, Mr. Hassall. I'll see he gets the message."

Like hell, I would. Things were still nice and quiet in the Albion when I hung up and moved out, and it looked as though I had my latest project all nicely bottled up. Bert Boggis, it transpired, was out on a job. In the ordinary run, for a hot potato like this one, I'd have pursued him all over the shop, but the urgency was dropping a bit, which explains in a roundabout way why I didn't see him till next day, in the sylvan setting of Gresham Park. And if you're wondering how I managed to have the ingot with me on that occasion, that's easily explained. I called *en route* for my usual hour with Stella. She'd tucked the ingot in the store cupboard and while she wasn't looking, I snitched it. I didn't think she'd notice the loss, and I meant to have it back in place before Billy Miles went asking for it.

★ ★ ★

Once he'd decided to shift his backside and act, Bert Boggis made short work of the Bragg-Norton affair. He introduced me to a detective inspector from the next door Force, we talked, and then they set the scene. I sneaked back to the Albion, trumped up an excuse to have a quick coffee with Stella and while she wasn't looking slipped the ingot back into her cupboard.

At six o'clock spot on, just as Billy Miles got back from work, the detective inspector rang the Albion Hotel and asked to speak to Miles. He explained he was ringing on behalf of Dominic Hassall and was looking to strike a bargain over some silver. True to form, Stella was at Billy's elbow and she grabbed the phone and insisted there was only one ingot under discussion. But I'd primed the D.I. about that, and he took it all in his stride.

By eight o'clock the trap was sprung. Billy Miles had flogged the silver — all fifty ingots of it, naturally — to a young detective posing as Hassall's man, and he was on his way to a cool cell at Mortley Main Police Station.

Poor old Dominic Hassall must have felt brassed off about it all. When Stella confided in me, some days later, I had to pretend I wasn't that much interested. It seems though, that half an hour after the D.I's call, somebody else came on the line, asking for Miles and babbling on about wanting to buy some silver. Stella took the call, and in her inimitable way she gave him no time to explain himself. She just sent him packing with a big flea in his ear. A few weeks later, I got my rake-off from the Bragg-Norton silver job, and I'll go so far as to say that it was a damned sight more than Bert's 'few quid'. Whereupon I forgot about the job — till this day, in Vince Skinner's caff.

And now I was talking to Detective Constable Warburton, who'd been the stooge buyer. And Warburton was trying to sell me something very different.

3

"GOOD day to you, Mr. Warburton," I said, risking a matey grin now that I could see who I was talking to. "I'm a fair-minded sort of bloke, and since you've unmasked I'll do the same. I do have a passing acquaintance wih the bold Bert Boggis, and on a couple of occasions I have put the odd little matter his way. Only as a public-spirited citizen, you understand, and only to help justice to prevail. I wouldn't want you thinking I was a full-time bounty hunter, or anything like that."

"We're on the same side, Peeper," Warburton said, evidently being more convinced about that than I was. "I wouldn't bother you with this job at all, only it's something I can't do myself, so I got to have somebody I can trust.

You'd be giving me a leg-up, as well as doing your duty — and you wouldn't have no need to worry about expenses."

He winked as he said that, I'm glad to say. You get a bit huffy about money in my profession, and if anybody starts talking about reimbursing bus fares the old ego tends to shrivel. But this bloke Warburton was making it plain he was talking about money in the wider sense. Maybe not the sort of wages to which I'd grown accustomed, and I wouldn't have expected that, because he was only a lad, struggling up towards the bigger leagues, but money in the sense of something back for services rendered. It did occur to me to ask *how much*, but I stifled my mercenary responses, kept my face friendly and my ear cocked.

"So do we talk business, Peeper?" He wondered.

"We do if you keep your voice down," I said, casting a wary glance round Vince Skinner's shoddy emporium. "I ain't all that keen on commercials." He nodded and went on in a whisper:

"But you're game for a try?"

"Hell, yes. I'm game for anything. What had you got in mind?"

"Let's leave the details for a bit. It's early days yet, and I just wanted to sound you out. We got to have a long talk about it, maybe tomorrow sometime. Where can we get together?"

"Not in this place, that's for sure. There's too many of the wrong sort get in here. Between you and me, Mr. Warburton, I find cars are best. You can park a car in any old place that suits, and they're not easily bugged. But motor bikes, now, they're neither use nor an ornament. Besides, I can't say I fancy riding pillion."

"I can get a car. That's easy. So name your place."

I named a quiet little lane down by the river, where not even a squirrel could sneak up on you without flashing its brush. It seemed he knew the place. He nodded his sweaty head.

"Ten o'clock tomorrow, then."

"Make it half past, Mr. Warburton."

"Fair enough. Half past it is. And don't keep calling me Mr. Warburton, please. The name's Eric."

"Right ho, Eric."

"And for the Lord's sake, Peeper, not a word about this to Sergeant Boggis. He doesn't know I'm talking to you at all. I wouldn't like him to think I was poaching on his preserves."

"You and me both," I said with feeling.

★ ★ ★

And at that, he almost walked away, but I hadn't finished with him yet. I cast a plain glance towards his globe-headed and anonymous mate who was still propping up Skinner's counter. He couldn't have been drinking tea, not with that brown vizor still blocking off his face, unless Vince had supplied him with a straw.

"You'll be coming on your own, I trust?"

51

"Don't worry about him," Warburton said with another knowing wink. "He's green, and he hasn't a clue what we're talking about."

"I noticed you never brought him over. That's good. But we really should trust each other, Eric. I'd like to know who he is."

"Stop bothering, man. He's one of my colleagues, that's all."

"You mean to say he's another copper?"

"Yes. A uniform man, new in the job. I just told him I wanted a private chat with an old mate. He thinks I'm wasting a bit of time."

"Maybe that's exactly what you're doing, Eric. Wasting my time as well as yours. But we'll have a better idea when I know what the job is."

★ ★ ★

If you want to know, I didn't feel a bit uneasy about that conversation with friend Warburton. Far from it — I was a hell of a lot uneasy. To begin with, I didn't much like the man. My feelings had nothing to do with his eyes being too close together, his chin being weak or one nostril being larger than the other. They weren't. In fact you might say he was quite a handsome bloke — not that I'm any judge of that sort of thing — and he looked sort of fit and well cared for, even if that leather suit did give him an appearance of the Michelin Man. And when I thought back over what he'd said, I couldn't fault him much on that score. He'd been polite, sensible, filled with earnest reason and half-way convincing. A bit pushing, maybe, but he was a jack after all. And still, I didn't like him.

For one thing he was too young and inexperienced to come making direct advances to a seasoned snout like me. It would have been a different matter entirely if I'd offered my services to him — or if he'd been satisfied with dropping a few gentle hints — but to come barging in like that with a full-blooded offer of work, on the strength of one previous casual meeting, seemed — well, it seemed wrong somehow. I felt like a blushing virgin who'd been flashed at. He was asking me to dance and propositioning me like mad in the same breath space. And it isn't easy crossing your legs in the middle of your first dance with a stranger. Warburton was on the make in the worst way. He'd sized me up as a good prospect and he was fancying his slice.

That angle made me resentful. It irked me that Warburton should have had the gall to try muscling in on my business relationship with Bert Boggis. You're thinking, I don't doubt, that I haven't found many nice things so far to say about Bert — and if you stand by, you'll hear me not saying a lot more nice things — but when you have a long-standing agreement going with somebody — when you're spoken for — the need for loyalty tends to creep in, and you don't feel disposed to kick your partner in the horrible, scraggy shins, or in the misplaced, antisocial balls.

Which is not to say that I'm the truest and most reliable of friends to anybody, or that I wouldn't have considered a spare bit on the side if it had been nice and clean and nothing said about it to annoy Bert, but I didn't think Warburton was nice and clean in any but the soap and water sense, and I certainly wasn't in a mood to be seduced.

Right at the heart of things, my not liking Warburton made me very wary indeed, as you always have to be if you make a living the way I do. There's no telling what people will get up to, and no knowing why they get up to it. Maybe Detective Constable Eric Warburton was only making his way in the world and trying to better himself. Maybe at the same time he was trying to better me. But just for the sake of debate, suppose he had something very unexpected up his sleeve? Suppose he had a down on people like me? Suppose Warburton was a secret card-carrying member of the Civil Rights Brigade? Suppose he was setting a trap? And for another thing, suppose I wasn't to be the bait, but the mouse?

All of which gave me pause, as a much cleverer bloke than me has been known to observe. But I was equal to the problem and I had a fair idea of how I was going to tackle it. This was plainly not an item for the floppy ears of Bert Boggis, so I meant to keep him right out of it except as a fount of information. I would play Warburton along, at least as far as meeting him tomorrow and listening to whatever he proposed to tell me. Whatever line I took after that, would depend on what he had to say. Meantime, it would do no harm at all to make myself better acquainted with the presumptuous detective — not to mention his mystery chum.

They walked out of Skinner's caff

without a backward glance, that monstrosity of a head cover having found its way back onto Warburton's bonce. I stayed put till the door closed on them, then I nipped over to the window and peeked out. I only had time to take one of the numbers off one of the bikes, and you can bet I didn't bother with Warburton's. I knew for sure who he was. It was the other bloke I wanted to check up on. I kept saying that number over in my mind on my way back to the table, and then, when nobody was looking, I wrote it down on the inside of my cigar packet. Ten minutes later, I was in a phone kiosk on a quiet corner with the business tackle to my ear, and Boggis was on the other end.

"You must be bonkers, Peeper," he said, friendly like.

"How's that, Bert?"

"I can't do things like this. You're asking me to misuse the Police Computer. You surely don't think this piece of valuable and highly sophisticated equipment can be used by all and sundry?"

"Suit yourself, Bert. But let's put it this way. One good turn deserves another — and vice versa. You better breathe in my ear, chum, or don't expect the benefit of my hot breath."

"You're a cruel bastard, Peeper. But hang on there for a minute while I bend the rules and put my job in jeopardy."

I had to wait more than a minute, but not much more, and it was a different Bert Boggis who came back on the line. All the officious pomposity had gone from him. He sounded cagey and suspicious, and he was bloody inquisitive.

"Well, well. It's odd company you're keeping these days."

"You've got the gen for me, Bert?"

"Oh I've got the gen all right. We very seldom fail."

"Go on then. Spit it out."

"Not so fast, old mate, old chum. Why should I tell you anything? What the hell do you want to know for?"

"Mind your own business."

"Oh very nice. So that's the way of things, is it? Well it's not good enough, Peeper. If you think for a minute I'm going to . . . "

"For God's sake, Bert, stop acting the goat. I'm here with a pen in my hand, so quit stalling and let's have it."

"His name's Harker. Shaun Harker. He lives at twenty-nine Seville Street. He's a right little hook is this one, Peeper. He's got form for screwing and wounding and . . . "

"You can leave it out, Bert. I know Harker better than you do. He's a scruffy little sod. I have to scratch myself every time I see him and I wouldn't trust him with the price of a pint. Thanks, Bert. You've done me a great job."

"Thanks nothing. That's my obligation met, and now it's your turn. What's your interest in young Harker?"

"You'd have a hell of a surprise if I

told you," I said, "but rest easy Bert. I've no intention of telling you."

He didn't swear or rant or anything. Not that I heard, anyway. But maybe that was because I slammed the phone down, quick, as soon as I'd finished speaking.

As they say in the best stories, I was busy with my thoughts. I ask you — a copper and an eighteen-carat fleece-lined shitbag of a young crook in open cahoots? That was puzzle enough, but it was only a small part of my worries. At first blush it could be argued that all I'd discovered was a young policeman with an abysmal choice in mates, but there was a hell of a lot more to it than that. Here was direct evidence that the pushful Mr. Warburton was a glib liar. *A colleague*, he'd said. *Another copper. A young man fresh signed up in the uniform branch*. Well, Shaun Harker wasn't any of those things and Eric Warburton knew damned well he wasn't. With a record like Harker's, they'd never have let him get his hands on an application form in case he nicked it. I hadn't seen Harker's face, but I didn't waste time wondering if maybe it wasn't him. It had to be him — else if the mystery bloke was really a copper, what was he doing riding a knock-off motor bike?

Tut, tut to Warburton. So far as I knew, he wasn't committing any real crime by knocking about with a tearaway, but it wasn't the done thing for a copper. Not in his bosses' eyes, or my eyes, or anybody else's eyes. If he'd confessed to having a bent mate — an old school chum who happened to have gone wrong — I could have found it in my heart to make allowances. But he'd told roasting lies about it, and that marked him down in my book as a rogue.

But there was another aspect of this cock-up, a much more serious aspect altogether. I knew Shaun Harker very well, and Harker knew me very well. I couldn't say for certain, but it seemed a fair bet that Warburton knew that I knew that Harker knew and so on, *ad infinitum*, if you see what I mean. Yet, with all that he knew, Warburton had brought Harker with him to the Golden Roof Restaurant (Skinner's caff to you) and with Harker looking on, he'd singled me out for a long conversation. Oh, I know Warburton had assured me that his mate, Harker, didn't know what we were talking about, but it was fairly obvious now that that had been another lie. All the time Warburton was chatting to me, Harker must have been looking on, knowing me. KNOWING ME, the bastard! And he'd made sure I didn't recognize him by the simple trick of keeping his swede locked away in that flaming great riding helmet. I hadn't much liked the helmet bit at the time. It just didn't seem natural that a bloke would spend half an hour in a caff, presumably having refreshments of some sort, and never even take his helmet off. Now I knew why the clever bugger had done it.

Harker must know everything about

me, why I was happy to talk to a copper and what we were talking about. By natural progression it probably followed that he knew about my little running arrangement with Bert Boggis. If he hadn't known about that before, he'd know now, all right. Warburton would have told him everything.

Because Warburton was bent — and for reasons that I couldn't begin to work out, he'd blown my cover wide open.

I took the realization very seriously, I can tell you. If Harker, or Warburton, or both decided to broadcast little snippets about me and my activities I could easily finish up out of business. And following that through, I began to sweat a little.

If the whisper got through to the wrong people, I could finish up dead.

4

WHATEVER in the name of God was I to do?

It's no use pretending I didn't contemplate flight, because I did, but I didn't contemplate it for very long. I've got two special facets in my nature that fight like billy-o with each other. One of them is curiosity and the other cowardice. These two have their fierce little battles on a regular basis and one of them always beats the other. The first time cowardice wins you'll know about it, because you'll see me catching a plane for Buenos Aires or Rio de Janeiro and there'll be an opening for a new snout to move in on Bert Boggis's payroll.

This time I decided I couldn't afford the fare, and at ten o'clock the next morning, if you'd been looking, you'd have seen me under an elderberry bush about a quarter of a mile from the place where I'd arranged to meet Detective Constable Warburton. I was just standing there, chewing a piece of grass while I waited. You think a quarter of a mile is a hell of a long way? Well, so it is, but that only goes to show how easy it is to be too clever for your own good.

I'd picked the spot for the meeting with an eye to privacy. It was at the end of a long strip of muddy track, the tail-end of a lane that ran from an old mill up by the river bridge, and it was at the point where the lane finally petered out. You could, in theory, approach the place from the opposite end, but only by wading through marshy land for about five miles, so for all practical purposes the lane was the only way in. With the river running along one side and the fence of a big factory along the other, there was no room for anybody to move in close without being spotted. Making it hard for other people, I'd made it hard for myself, but I sure as hell wasn't going to be seen meeting Warburton till I'd made sure it was going to be Warburton and nobody else.

The elderberry bush I'd chosen was hard by the approach road and he'd have to pass me in order to keep the appointment. I was looking down on the road, so I knew I'd have a good view of him — and his passengers, if any — as he went by. If he came alone, as he'd agreed, I was prepared to go through with it up to a point, but if he had Harker or anybody else with him, he could go stuff himself.

He arrived in a little Ford Escort, about twenty-five past ten and I craned my neck as the car went past. Warburton was at the wheel and the other seats were empty. If Harker had come along for the ride he had to be in the boot, and that I didn't believe. I hung on a bit after he'd gone, just in case some motor bike or other happened to come sneaking along behind him, but there was no sign, so I set off walking and got to the spot right on half past. Warburton had picked a dry patch and was sitting in the car. He leaned over and shoved the passenger door open.

"Nice timing, Peeper," he said, giving me a wide grin. I nodded and bared my teeth, but hung back.

"You're pointing the wrong way, chum," I told him. "So do a nice little three-pointer and then we'll start."

"There's no need for that, Peeper. There's nobody around."

"Do it — or I piss off. You takes your choice."

After he'd turned the car, I climbed in. It was positioned more or less as I wanted it. Looking straight out through the front screen gave me a good view of the approach road as far as the bush where I'd first waited, and I reckoned if anything moved at that distance I could be out, over the fence and off through the factory buildings before even a motor bike could reach me.

"You satisfied now?" Warburton

said, a bit sarcastic.

"That's fine, Eric. You got my full attention."

"All right then. But first off, I want to show you something."

Warburton reached inside his jacket and took out a brown leather wallet. I eyed it with considerable interest, because if there was anything in the way of reward coming to me, his wallet was the likeliest source. It looked convincingly fat and while he was fiddling through it I caught the friendly flash of blue and green that has always been one of my favourite visions. But the wallet wasn't open long. A quick flip and it was back in his pocket. The thing he handed me was a snapshot, one of those thick, instamatic colour prints. I took it off him and looked at it.

"Do you recognize that bloke?"

It wasn't a top class photograph but there was ample detail for me to make my mind up. The chap was stocky and red-faced, with dark hair, receding at the temples, and a straggly moustache in a lighter colour. His outfit was sober and conventional, a dark two-piece suit, white shirt, collar and tie and shiny black shoes. I looked hard at the face. It rang no bells with me.

"Not at a quick glance," I told him.

"A quick glance isn't good enough, Peeper. Photographs can put you right off sometimes. Have a real good look at him and think."

I peered a bit closer.

"I might have passed him in a bus queue, or at the Bookie's Office, but if I ever did, I don't remember. He isn't somebody I've ever chatted with, that's for sure."

"Is there a chance he might know you?"

"Oh do give over, Eric. How the hell do I answer that?"

"No, I suppose you can't. But this is very important, Peeper, because if he's likely to recognize you, the deal's off."

"The deal better be off then, because I can't say yea or nay."

"But at least you've had no sort of dealings with that bloke?"

"No, not a chance. I've a good memory for faces, and if I'd as much as stood next to him having a pint, I'd have remembered."

Warburton sat ruminating and I waited. After a minute or so he took the snap back off me and tucked it in alongside the wallet.

"So you're good at faces, are you? Does that mean you'd be able to recognize that man if you should see him again?"

"Yes, so long as he looks anything like his picture. Mind you, if he was togged out as Father Christmas it might be difficult."

"Don't worry. That's the way he'll look. Well that's it then, Peeper. I got to take a chance on it. Do you know the Green Man?"

"The Green Cross Code bloke, or the Jolly Green Giant?"

"Neither, clever bugger. I mean the pub in Harcourt Street."

"Oh, that place. Well, yes and no. I had a pint there once, but I didn't like the beer or the pub, so I moved on."

"You're not likely to be recognized if you go there?"

"This is beginning to bother me, Eric," I said, frowning.

"Unless I know when I'm going there, and who's going to be in, how the hell can I say? And aren't you stretching things just a bit? I'm not a copper after all and I hope nobody knows I even speak to coppers, so what do you think anybody's going to recognize me *as*? I'm recognized in a lot of places, but only as a bloke who happens to live in these parts, and I shouldn't think that would make any odds."

There was another bout of silence while he considered the case.

"You've got a point, Peeper. I don't suppose it does matter a lot. Only

71

if you should happen to meet an acquaintance, play it crafty. Even if it means you can do this little job for me."

"I'm always careful, Eric. I know how these things go. But a lot depends on the nature of this little job of yours. Isn't it time we stopped fencing and got down to some straight talking?"

"I want you to go to the pictures," he said.

Well, I've heard some curious things in my time, but that just about took first prize. I gave him a look of amazement. If I say I was aghast, that describes my feelings better.

"You're pulling my leg, Eric. I haven't been to the flicks twice since I was a kid. It isn't in my line. But I do remember it's always dark in those places, so how do I see what I'm looking for?"

"I'm not talking about that sort of cinema. Tell me, Peeper, are you squeamish at all? Do you go all prudish when they mention sex? Would it upset you to sit in on a couple of blue films?"

"I might even enjoy it, Eric. But where's the catch? And what the hell have blue films got to do with the Green Man? Oh, I think I get it now. It's colour code. I'm to watch for a negro flogging yellow submarines to a Red Indian — is that it?"

"All right, Peeper, you can cut out the comedy. If you'll pin your ears back I'll explain. The man in the picture is Denzil Conway. He's a tit-and-bum merchant in a biggish way. He runs the best hard porn films on a home projector and he sells tickets at the Green Man. He's a perverted bastard — and I want him."

I didn't say anything for a while, because I was doing my sums. I was beginning to understand the plot by this time, but I was seeing a flaw in it all — a hell of a flaw, from my point of view. Quite honestly, I don't give a damn who chooses to purvey muck, or how, or when, or where, so long as they don't blame me for it. I'm not your tuppenny moralist who fights crime for the good of his own soul; I'm in it for the money; and it follows that I mainly involve myself in those cases that have an end to their rainbow. They say there's plenty of money in blue films and I don't doubt there is, but I wasn't being invited to share the spoils — I was being sent in to stop it happening — and for the life of me I couldn't see where the profit was in the job. You put the cops onto a load of valuable gear and you click for a nice reward, but help the cops to shut down a sleazy film club and where does it get you?

But my fortune comes in fits and starts. I still had half a nest egg from my last pay-out and I wasn't going to starve for a week or two. And like I said before, I have this strong sense of curiosity. So I resisted the temptation to climb out and walk away, mainly because Warburton and his weary story intrigued me. "I thought porn was more or less legal these days?"

"A lot of it is, Peeper, in the right circumstances. But from what I hear, the stuff Conway peddles is real turgid. And the point is, he's operating in a private dwelling-house and charging top rate for viewing. That puts him on the wrong side of all sorts of little laws."

"Even so, I shouldn't have thought a detective would have been mad keen to chase up that sort of case."

"You mustn't get me wrong. If it was just porn, I'd leave it to the porn boys. But there's something else; something a damned sight nastier; and that's where you come in."

"Go on. I'm a big boy. I can stand it."

Warburton leaned towards me in a conspiratorial way and switched on a look that reeked of sincerity.

"Drugs," he said. "All kinds of poisonous muck. Not just the odd joint, but the hard stuff. The stuff that kills."

I was a bit more interested, but not much. If you want my philosophy, I don't like drugs and I'd have them banned except for true medicinal purposes. But there's a time and place for philosophy and this wasn't it. Where was the money? I've heard all these stories about drug hauls that are worth God knows how many millions on the streets, but that's only if you happen to be selling the stuff. I've never heard of anybody being paid vast sums for assisting with recovery. Still, I don't know everything about everything and there might be a profit I'd never even thought of. I decided to stay with the game.

"Sounds like a job for a big team," I suggested.

"Are you kidding! This is my job, Peeper, and I intend to stick to it. We may have to go mob-handed in the end, but by the time I break it open I want it parcelled up so tight that nobody can claim it but me."

He was snapping a bit. It sounded

as though I'd touched him on the raw. But he was switched through to my wavelength there. During a long association with Bert Boggis I'd come across this professional rivalry bit quite regularly. Boggis never openly discussed it with me, but I can remember him crowing to some tune when he'd managed to slip in and pinch a case off a brother officer. And if it happened the other way round, as it often did, the old Boggis *bonhomie*, always a tender flower, would welter in death throes for weeks. So I could easily understand how young Warburton would want to keep a nice little set-up all to himself, and to that extent I sympathized with him. Whether I was prepared to put myself out just to help him stitch up a case was a question of a different order.

"You seem to know a hell of a lot about Conway already," I pointed out. "Why don't you just call in yourself at the Green Man, tail him home and shove your warrant card in his hand?"

"I can't, Peeper. Damn it, man, I told you at the outset that this was a job I couldn't do personally. That pub's a right den of thieves. The minute a cop walks in there they can smell him. And they don't need even noses to know when I go in. Half the customers in there have had my hand on their collars."

"Send somebody else in then. Somebody they don't know."

Detective Constable Eric Warburton was very disappointed in me. I could tell by the look in his eyes and by the way he sagged in his seat and got ready to be sick.

"Christ Almighty, Peeper. Haven't you been listening at all? Send somebody in they don't know! What the hell do you suppose I've been trying to do for the last half hour?"

There was no answer to that, so I didn't try to give one. But I still hadn't got the thing fully sorted out in my mind.

"You know he's running blue movies,"

78

I said, "and you know he's hawking drugs. So will you please explain to me how much better off you'll be after I attend a session. When I come out, I tell you they're showing blue movies and hawking drugs. And you say, *What the hell! I knew that already*."

"If it was like that, Peeper, you wouldn't be sitting in my car. I've got a fair bit of dirt, granted, but I need a lot more. I want to be strong. I want confirmation at first hand of all the rumours I've been hearing. I want to know what the precise set-up is in Conway's house: which rooms he uses for what purposes; what time he puts the shows on and who projects; how the drugs get peddled, where they're stored, how they're delivered. In other words, the whole shooting match. And in particular, I want to know the part Conway plays in all this. How he flogs the tickets, how much he charges, whether he handles the drugs himself. It's Conway I'm after. Just him. I'm not too bothered about the rest of the ragtag and bobtail who get in there. I want a good strong case against Conway. When I raid that house, I want to be able to grab Conway without saying a dicky bird, chuck him in a cell and tell him how he operates, without having to depend on him telling me. Now I've stuck my neck out with you, Peeper. I've told you a hell of a lot of stuff that I wouldn't tell anybody who wasn't on my side. And I'm counting on you to come through. So can I take it we've got a deal?"

"How do I break into this circle of vice?"

"You drop in at the Green Man, have a few beers, suck up to Conway and let him take you on from there. Get a ticket, go to one of his shows, keep your eyes open and report back to me."

"Who buys the beer? Who pays for the ticket?"

"I do."

He dragged his wallet out, peeled

off three fivers and held them out to me. I didn't take it straight away. It wasn't that fifteen quid wouldn't do for starters — hell, I've known Bert Boggis palm me off with just a couple of quid — but I had my own thoughts about the cost of tickets for a show of the sort Conway was supposed to be involved in. I wasn't entirely convinced that I should touch the job at all, but if I did, I wanted the financial side to be well established.

"That's peanuts for porn movies," I said.

"I don't think so. You've got to remember, this is a working class district with a lot of folk on the dole. Anyway, there's plenty more where that came from. If you have to go over the top, I'll straighten up with you after."

"You want me to subsidize you? Christ, Eric, you've got a nerve. And never mind the expenses — what about something in the pot for me, when the job's over?"

"I pay on results," Warburton said enigmatically.

★ ★ ★

And there it was. With a great mess of reservations still troubling me, I told Warburton I'd take the job. And as he stopped to drop me out just short of the main road I very nearly changed my mind. But I didn't. I walked away from him, regretting my decision and wishing I'd never met Warburton. I hoped like mad that Boggis would never find out. Not just because he'd know I was cheating on him, which was bad enough of itself, but also because he'd damn me for a thousand kinds of fool. If there was one golden rule that Bert Boggis insisted on in all our dealings, and that he kept ramming down my throat at every opportunity, it was *Don't get involved. If you keep your nose clean you'll be all right*, he'd say. *But if you get yourself mixed up in any shady deals and you get yourself*

82

arrested, I won't lift a finger to help you. I'll even knock you off myself.

Good advice. Damned good advice. And yet here I was, on the say-so of a young unblooded jack, proposing to join up with a gang of drug pushers and porn merchants. Come to think of it, I didn't require Boggis to point out the folly of what I was doing. I could see it all too clearly myself.

But I was in too deep to wriggle out easily. And anyway, I was under an obligation to young Warburton. I'd taken his money, piffling amount though it was, and I do have a sort of professional integrity that keeps urging me to play straight with people.

Besides, I'd never seen a real, honest-to-goodness filthy picture, and it might turn out to be a lot of fun.

5

WORMING my way into Denzil Conway's confidence — and into his house — took four evenings, and in that time I spent a damned sight more than the fifteen quid sub., I'd collected from Warburton. But I mustn't get too far ahead of myself.

I went in the Green Man that first night and didn't enjoy it very much. The place was full of unpleasant odours that seemed to suggest unwashed bodies or an unwashed pub, or both. In fact, it stank a man's height, and the ale was a strange and very unsavoury brew. But I warmed to my task and sucked up to the deadliest collection of cut-throats and perverts you could possibly imagine. As far as I could tell, nobody knew me, and I knew nobody to speak to, although I spoke to one or two as the evening progressed. I stayed right through till closing time, got myself half cut and went home feeling that the world owed me something and had refused to settle.

Doreen wasn't best pleased, but I'd been in her good books for quite some time and it takes more than the odd boozing session to really get her dander up. So she didn't chuck me out. In fact we got a bit lovey-dovey eventually, and that helped to cheer me up.

I've mentioned Doreen before. She lives in a neat little terraced house on the outskirts of the town, and that's where I live too, most of the time. Doreen's just about the best thing that ever happened to me and if ever I decide to get married, which I sure as hell won't if I can help it, she'll get first refusal. Because what a man needs in a wife is a good cook, a chatty and sympathetic companion, somebody very nice to look at and a kindred spirit when it comes to getting the best out of bed in bed. You won't have forgotten Stella, and I must say Stella meets some of those criteria, but Doreen is all of those things and more. She was just a kid when I first met her, a lovely, lively, sexy kid, and as the years go by she seems to improve in all categories. Being a spitting hell-cat, as she can certainly be, makes for a stormy spell now and then. And because God gave her more muscles than any woman is properly entitled to, whenever we fight she always wins. But that only adds sparkle to our relationship and I wouldn't like a placid little cow half so much.

But enough about Doreen. On my second trip to the Green Man I got a bit nearer to Conway. I'd seen him on my first visit and had no difficulty in recognizing him, but I only saw him fleetingly, because he seemed to bob about the place like a sparrow in a field of breadcrumbs. On this second night I bought a few beers for a rough-looking mixed bunch and Conway joined us for about five minutes. Nothing said, nothing done, and I'm too old a bird to show my hand by making approaches, but Conway spared me a glance or two and I got the distinct impression that he was sizing me up.

On the third night I collected a few *hellos* and it seemed I was coming to be regarded as a new member. Later that evening, the bunch I was with started to talk dirty. Only the usual sex jokes at first, and I enjoy good, funny sex jokes as much as any man, but the talk moved on, the Port Said portraits came out and there were broad hints of better things to come. You can sense progress if you try, and I was sensing it good and strong.

I let myself go a bit on the fourth night, and after they called 'time' I was favoured with an invitation to stay on a bit. Nothing new in that, of course. Permitted hours are just a game in some pubs. The landlord puts jam on his bread by flogging a bit extra to trusted friends, after time, behind closed doors and shuttered windows, but you have to break into the circle before he'll tip you the wink. That fourth night it seemed I'd been mixing with the right people and giving them the right impressions, because I was still inside when they locked the door.

After that, the whole atmosphere in the Green Man became sort of conspiratorial and Conway was treating me like a long-lost brother. I'd seen him at other times, flitting from place to place and whispering in people's ears, but he'd avoided me pretty pointedly so far. Now, with the ice crackling and melting all around me, he sidled up and shoved a double whisky in my hand. I gave him a *cheerio* and after a decent interval sent him a pint over, not wishing to seduce him onto the hard stuff. When he brought the second double whisky, he also brought his proposition.

There was a bit of a stag do arranged, it seemed. A few of the lads were going off to see a show — the sort of show that you could only describe with nudge-nudges and a broad leer.

Of course you had to be a real sport to appreciate what was on the menu, and the least said about it the better. Moreover, these little displays cost the earth and it was only fair that if you cut yourself in you had to fork out something towards the hiring fee. I listened to him very carefully, drooled a bit, made the right noises and found myself part of the queue.

It cost me a tenner. To be honest, I baulked a bit at that, but I didn't crack on, and I passed the two blues over without a murmur, making a mental note to screw it back out of Warburton, with interest, the first chance I got. Looking around my motley companions I couldn't help wondering how many of them managed to go more than once at those prices, But I suppose there are more funny people around than ever you realize.

They had it arranged very nicely. No tickets. Well, that went without saying. When Warburton had first mentioned tickets I'd accepted it as a figure of speech, and it was. We left the pub in dribs and drabs. Conway's house was only a short distance and although there were quite a few cars in the car-park, everybody went on foot. They had the damnedest system for letting people in. The commercial entrance was through a little porch to the back door. There was a bright light in the porch. You had to knock three times, sharply. I wouldn't have known that, but the bloke who went with me had the system off. After the knock, there was a short delay before the door opened and you were allowed to creep in. I nearly missed the system, but I cottoned on as I was closing the door. There was one of those tiny little telescopes screwed through the door, a device about half an inch diameter that you can peep through to see who's knocking. That might present a bit of an obstacle for Warburton, so I bore it in mind.

Conway's living quarters were evidently

dead ahead, but there was a middle-aged, horse-faced woman — the one who'd let us in, I supposed — blocking that door and pointing the way up a flight of stairs. She didn't ask any questions; didn't do or say anything else; which seemed to augur well for Warburton's official visit.

Denzil Conway himself was standing at the top of the stairs, hurrying us along and fending us in through a door. I expected to walk into a bedroom, but he must have had a mate in the building trade, because what I found was two big bedrooms chopped into one. I could see the big rolled steel girder vaulting across the ceiling where the dividing wall had originally been. Superficially, the place was like one of those modern Unit Four picture houses, but nothing like so plush. There was a biggish screen at one end and a projector at the other. The chairs were rickety wooden things — school chairs — and there was a lot of crashing and creaking as people settled into their places.

The room was maybe a quarter full when I got there and as I waited it filled up to about half capacity. That seemed to be all they were expecting, because Conway left his post at the stairhead and walked through to fiddle with the projector.

While he was getting things ready, I had a good look round at my fellow patrons of vice and lechery. Most of them I'd seen before in the Green Man, but I reckoned there was a fair sprinkling of outsiders. I was pleased to see no familiar faces. Damn it all, that sort of thing wasn't my scene. I couldn't help feeling guilty and besmirched and I don't like friends seeing me in that condition. Generally speaking though, the rest of the customers seemed to be waiting in eager anticipation — and some of them were grey-haired old fogeys who ought to have known better. I didn't think they'd be too deeply into drugs, so for that angle I concentrated on the dozen or so younger, leather-jacketed oafs who had banded together in one corner at the back of the room. I could smell grass — oh yes, I know what cannabis smells like — and I noticed the odd joint being passed around like a pipe of peace, but I looked in vain for any sign of the hard stuff. Still, I thought, if there was any of it about, that was where it was most likely to be found.

The hubbub settled down, the lights dimmed and we were off on our titillating voyage. I don't know if you've ever seen a blue film, or if I'm treading on anyone's toes when I say they aren't much cop, but I watched the first one pretty closely because it was a new experience for me. Some of the cavorting was new to me as well — imaginative, if you know what I mean — but I honestly didn't learn any new positions that I felt like adding to my repertoire. The film opened with a lot of numbered frames, all higgledy-piggledy, and then a pair of enormous boobs appeared before me and as the camera moved away to reveal the rest of their buxom and voluptuous owner, the title came up.

BIG GIRL IN A BLACK NIGHTIE. But she wasn't. She was mother naked and she had the thickest, darkest patch of pubic hair I've ever seen in my life. I can tell you now, that no black nightie was ever featured in the whole episode. The nearest I saw to clothing was a pair of black nylons, a pair of black suspenders and a tiny little maid's apron, all five worn by a damsel of passing fair appearance who served drinks halfway through (on the film, I mean. There wasn't so much as a biscuit served to the patrons) and stayed to have herself mounted in succession by two tubby white blokes and a large man of darker pigment, which is the best description I can give without being accused of racial discrimination.

There was no dialogue and none necessary. Both women and one of the men were very well made indeed. I felt a bit sorry for the other two men, though they say there's many a good tune played on a little whistle, and I must say they got where they wanted to go at least a couple of times. But there's a limit to how many times, and I don't give a damn who disagrees with me. And speaking for myself, there's also a limit to how much of this stuff I can take before wanting to puke. They prolonged the proceedings a fair while with some very gymnastic manipulations and some interesting shots of the things your mother always warned you against, but before the film ended the Law of Diminishing Returns was weighing very heavily on me and I was thinking of all those better things I could have bought with my ten quid.

It was fairly obvious that everybody else didn't think like me. I listened to a great many *ooohs* and *aaahs*, not to mention a great deal of rhythmic creaking, and although I thought some of the shots were hilarious, nobody laughed. Far from it, the whole show was viewed in deadly seriousness. A fair sprinkling of the audience seemed to have developed a consuming interest in their trouser pockets and were scratching themselves furtively — some of them not so furtively.

Keeping my mind on the job, I noticed two other things which I thought I could usefully pass on to Warburton. At least half a dozen people came in late and creaked their way into spare chairs, so it was obvious they didn't lock the gates at the kick-off. The other thing concerned Conway. I was keeping a wary eye on him, as Warburton had suggested. Most of the time he stood by the projector, but at one stage, when he must have judged that everybody was looking elsewhere, I saw him sneak over to the group of youths and duck down in their midst. There was much fiddling and whispering. I never saw anything change hands, but I got the clear impression that something did. It might have been fags, or even iced lollies, but somehow I didn't think so. Well, it wasn't much to report, but it was something.

I nearly walked out on the second film. I would have walked out, but I knew that would only draw attention to me, and that I didn't want. It was a German film and like the first it was entirely without dialogue. In that case, how do I know it was German? Well, the title was KINDER LIEBE, and I'm not so ignorant that I don't know that's German, or that it roughly translates into CHILDREN LOVE, or something very like that. And that's exactly what it was about, assuming you read LOVE as SEX. Tiny little chits of girls getting up to the most disgusting tricks with a couple of fat-bellied grandfather figures. Mostly it was the usual things in both usual and unusual places, but they also did some questionable things with mirrors, milk-bottles and fountain pens. And, God help us, the kids seemed to enjoy it. At least, they had soppy grins on their faces whenever the camera homed in on faces from their preoccupation on other parts. But I didn't like it at all. I so strongly didn't like it that, given the chance, I'd have shot the bastards who'd made it. And I itched to deliver a kick in the balls to every bloke in that poky little hall who had the crust to appreciate such muck, which as far as I could see meant every other man jack except myself.

There was a third presentation, short, crude and completely untitled. Frankly, I don't think it was a pukka film at all; just a selection of poorly taken home movies with a series of podgy or painfully angular women having it off with bored looking men or, in a couple of cases, cumbersomely with each other. And by then, I was halfway to taking the pledge and giving up sex for life. I tell you, I was greatly relieved when the screen blacked out, the lights came on and we all shuffled out.

So you can keep your blue movies, friends, and much good may they do you. Anybody who wants the address of Denzil Conway's little picture palace would be well advised not to write to me.

But there was one further little interesting snippet which came as we were ready to leave. I don't mean interesting to me, I mean potentially interesting to D.C. Warburton. With a happy smile on his face, Conway called us all to attention to announce that the place would be in operation same time on the following night, and anybody who'd seen enough of tonight's showing (Lordy, Lordy, did he mean to say they showed those films more than once?) would be pleased to know that an entirely new programme was on offer. He wrapped his tongue round the titles with slavering gusto, advising us on no account to miss NURSIE LOVES NURSIE, CONFESSIONS OF AN OVERSEXED AU PAIR and NUN RAPE. I made a note in my mental diary — not to come within twenty miles of the place.

6

IT didn't work out as I intended. Things seldom do. As events were to transpire, when the time came I was right there outside the house — for reasons which I'll explain in due course.

I did a lot of thinking after I came out of Conway's porn parlour and said a cursory *good night* to my fellow voyeurs. There was a misty drizzle hanging over the town, but the air smelt wonderfully sweet and clean. Walking home, I tried to think of happier things than I'd just witnessed, but the memory kept coming back. I could have used a bath and a gargle if the means had been readily available.

It was well past midnight by then, and I knew it was no use chasing after Warburton at that hour, because the drill was that I reported to him the morning after. Even so, I was half tempted to go right away and knock him out of his bed.

All of a sudden I was firmly on Warburton's side. I was glad I'd been able to dig out the sort of information he needed and I couldn't wait to pass it on. Whether he ever gave me a decent rake-off — whether he even settled up for the money I'd already spent — didn't seem to matter much any more. I wanted him to raid that stinking place. I wanted him to drag Denzil Conway off in irons and chuck him into the coldest, clammiest cell he could find. And I wanted him to make it stick, so that Conway collected the heaviest sentence it was possible to impose. I even felt disposed to volunteer myself as a witness if he needed one, and that's something you must never do if you want to make the grade in my profession.

I hadn't entirely overcome my suspicion of young Detective Constable Warburton, or forgiven him for any of the dubious things he was obviously involved in, but I could see now that the job he'd pulled me into was a worthwhile job, something that deserved to be tackled and something that I was pleased to help with, even if the returns were poor. So I started making excuses for the man. Maybe his heart was in the right place after all? Maybe I should show a bit more confidence in him? Maybe even a cop was entitled to stick with a friend who wasn't quite so straight as himself?

I even made allowances for his lies, which turned out to be no difficult thing to do, because after all, if he was shackled to a mate of doubtful pedigree you could hardly expect him to go round bragging about it. I could see now that the lies Warburton had told had been white lies, designed to cover up his own embarrassment and at the same time avoid embarrassing me. And I gave him credit for truthfulness in the other areas that mattered. He really was to be trusted with a confidence. He really had kept his mouth shut about me and my dealings with himself and Bert Boggis. Shaun Harker, that snotty little ruffian, really was just an off-duty friend and not privy to any secrets Warburton had as a policeman.

So I was in cheery mood the next morning when I met Warburton at the appointed hour. And after I'd filled him in on all the detail I'd been able to pick up he seemed more than pleased with my efforts. He agreed at once that tonight was the night. He could hardly have done anything else, I suppose. We could say for sure that there would be a show tonight, and that was something we couldn't say about any other night. So, after we spent some time going over my story, he thanked me nicely and said it was all right to lay off. There wouldn't be any more shows, he assured me. There might be half of one, but there'd be an interruption ruder than the film, and then it would be curtains for Denzil Conway.

We came to the time of parting and

Warburton hadn't mentioned money at all. I didn't have the heart to remind him. Hell's bells, I really must be slipping.

★ ★ ★

After I left Warburton, I called in at the Albion Hotel with the intention of keeping Stella sweet, but I didn't stay long and we never even got as far as the boudoir. She wasn't all that pleased with me, but I stammered excuses and managed to get away in one piece. The truth was that thoughts of Conway and his dirty little den were still curling round in my head and putting me off. I thought about very little else for the rest of the day, and as boozing time came to fruit I wandered over towards the Green Man. Towards it only — you'll please note. No power on earth could have induced me to go in. But I found better beer in another pub not too far away. I was filled with joy, because Conway was about to get his come-uppance and I had an overwhelming desire to go and knit — or something — beside his gibbet. Whenever I have an overwhelming desire, as I do fairly frequently, I usually grab whatever the object is with both hands.

Which I hope explains why — as I told you earlier — I was parked outside Conway's place at the appointed hour.

★ ★ ★

You can always find somewhere to keep watch. I found a new house-building lot, almost directly opposite the porn shop. The place had several advantages. There was a wooden fence fronting the street and it completely shielded me from view. The street was well lighted, but the site wasn't, and the fence cast a long deep shadow which swallowed me up. There were several pairs of houses about a hundred yards to my rear and I could see lights in some of their windows, but a resident might have stared out of his window all night without seeing me. Best of all, there was a convenient chink in the fence which gave me a first-class view of the night's arena. It had one disadvantage too. I had to stand in soft, sloppy clay. But I'm too old and wise ever to look for perfection in anything.

At the cost of muddy shoes I had a grand-stand position, and I'd hardly had time to settle in and light a small cigar before the game got under way.

Conway was first to arrive and he came alone. The path to his back door was gloomy, but at its far end I could see rays of light coming from the porch which was just out of my vision. I watched him waddle up the path, turn left and pass from view. Within minutes, the *habitués* began to roll up; a group of three, a few singles, a pair, a party of half a dozen. I noticed that most of them came from the direction of the Green Man, but a few others came from the opposite direction; older men mainly; the greybeards I'd noticed at the session I attended. After a while there was a lull in the procession, then, at longer intervals, two or three others made their pilgrimage. The first seedy epic would have begun to roll by now, I judged, and I wondered in a detached way if they were watching nuns or nurses or *au pairs*. One thing I knew for certain, whichever category was screened first, their soft and secret parts would be under explicit attack.

And where was the relieving force in the shape of Eric Warburton and his merry men? They didn't show up at first, and I began to wonder if the scheme had suffered a hiccup. I also began to wonder — silly perhaps, but true — whether I'd slipped up in my choice of vantage point. For all I knew, Warburton might have decided to cordon the area and might have chosen this same building site on which to deploy some of his forces. Suppose half a dozen muscular coppers suddenly descended on this very spot and found me conducting my own observations?

What story could I possibly invent to explain my presence here? And if I failed to satisfy them, might I not finish up in a cell? The cell adjoining Conway's, perhaps?

Warburton's arrival stilled my fears. He came in the same Ford Escort and parked it in the street, about fifty yards short of Conway's house. I couldn't make out his face at that distance, but I could see two people in the car — Warburton and one other, I supposed. They would be the advance guard and the troops would close in behind, ready to block all exits while a chosen task force went in to carry out the arrests.

The two men stayed in the car for maybe five minutes, but if they waited for a back-up, they waited in vain. After that they climbed out and walked towards the house. They were properly kitted out for the job — both wearing rough-looking clothing and old-fashioned raincoats — dressed exactly as patrons of such a dive might be expected to appear. As they moved in I could see Warburton plainly; and then, when they were right up against Conway's front gate, I got a clear view of the second man. I recognized him straight off, but I couldn't begin to believe it.

Shaun Harker.

The two men walked up the path, turned left and disappeared. I was left watching a little car in an otherwise empty street.

Once I'd recovered from the shock I started making allowances again, but it was a damned sight harder this time. I'd already half forgiven Warburton for spending his off-duty time with a little gobshite like Harker, but taking him along on a police raid — that was stretching things a bit too far. The only remaining possibility, if the set-up could be rationalized at all, was that the relationship between Warburton and Harker was on all fours with that between me and Bert Boggis. Harker must be his snout — and because Warburton couldn't risk being recognized as a cop, he'd enlisted Harker to show his crooked face to the spyglass at the door and persuade the old woman to let both of them in.

There was a certain acceptable logic in that explanation, and although I suffered from a hundred lingering doubts I was moved to accept it, if only for the time being. I even allowed that he might have arranged a back-up, and that the extra hands might be stationed well back out of my sight. So I waited and watched, those being the only two things I could reasonably do.

I finished my cigar, dropped the butt and squelched the glowing end into the mud. And when I looked through the chink again, things had started to happen. The path beside Conway's house had become a parade of departing guests. They came out all of a ruck, deprived of raped nuns or sexy *au pair* girls or something, looking sheepish and muttering to each other. And once outside they split up, scattered and passed from view. The street was once more deserted, but I continued to wait. Warburton and Harker were still in there, with at the very least Conway and his woman, and I wondered what the hell they were doing. Maybe they hadn't found any drugs on this occasion? That certainly seemed to figure, because amongst the departing guests I seemed to remember all the leather-jacketed yobs. Maybe Conway had been tipped off? Maybe Warburton and Harker had burst in to find the screen filled with a spirited display by Laurel and Hardy? Either way, I was beginning to be bored, and just as I was about to say *the hell with it* and walk away, there was more movement.

Denzil Conway was led out, plainly under close arrest. The two men holding his arms were Warburton and Harker. Warburton, I could see, was holding three reels of film under his spare arm, which seemed to suggest that the nuns, the nurses and the *au pairs* had actually been on parade tonight. They shunted Conway along the street and tipped him into the Ford Escort. Warburton chucked the reels onto the back seat and they all climbed in. Harker was in the back with Conway, guarding him. The car was driven away.

I suppose I must be one of the world's great thinkers. I certainly had plenty to think about as I walked home. I'd come to see Conway knocked off and Warburton hadn't disappointed me, so to that extent the night had been well spent. But try as I might, I couldn't reconcile the way it had been done with what I'd always understood to be the norm. I half understood why only Conway had been arrested — I remembered Warburton saying very forcibly that it was Conway he wanted and not the others — but if there had been evidence of drug transactions I'd have expected him to gather in both seller and buyer. It wasn't enough to

112

believe that maybe the evidence had been missing, because he hadn't even gone there ready to find it. Two men didn't make a decent raid team. Quite clearly, Conway had been Warburton's only target from the start.

On top of all that, I felt foolishly jealous of Harker. I'd been in the grassing game longer than he had, and I'd found myself in some highly entertaining situations over the years.

But Bert Boggis had never allowed me to go with him and take part in an arrest.

* * *

At risk of being a dreadful bore, I'll mention again that I'm only on the fringe of the law and order business — the poacher turned gamekeeper — and I wouldn't be in the business at all if it wasn't for the money. The fact that in my latest venture I stood out of pocket was only a minor detail, since by the normal order of things

I don't expect to draw my wages till the job has been completely wrapped up — and sometimes not for a hell of a while after. That apart, and speaking in general terms, I lose all interest in a job once my part in it has ended.

But I couldn't forget the Conway case. It had some mighty curious features and it kept bugging me. I couldn't sleep that first night for worrying about it. I kept turning the details over in my mind, and by morning I'd come to a decision. I had to chase it through and see the final outcome, or I'd never rest easy again.

There are various ways of checking up on the progress of a case. The best of all — for me, that is — is to get on the blower to Bert Boggis and ask him what gives. You'll have gathered though, that in present circumstances I didn't have that facility. Oh, Bert could have found out all right — and he would have, if I'd twisted his arm — but without showing myself up for the cheating bastard I was,

I couldn't approach Bert. I might ask him in a casual way; pretend Conway was a mate of mine and I'd just heard about his trouble; but Bert can see farther than most blokes through a wood, and I had an uncomfortable feeling he'd see through me.

On first glance, there seemed to be no really good reason why I shouldn't approach the detective in the case. I had a telephone number to contact him, and he could hardly grumble, because in a sense he'd become a second string to my bow, but I had a little itchy feeling that warned me not to get further involved with friend Warburton. At least, not till the time was ripe for reminding him he owed me money.

So I'd have to use other means, and the next best means was to slip into court and collect a report at first hand. I'd appeared in the Dock a time or three, so maybe it was time I showed up in the Public Gallery. The risks involved were of no great consequence.

Somebody might see me there and put two and two together, but so what? It might surprise you to know that I'm no shrinking violet. Views differ about whether I'm a man or an insect, depending on which side of the fence you happen to stand, but one thing you can take for granted. I don't mind taking risks when I have to. When the spotlight shines, I don't crawl away and hide under a stone. If it were otherwise, I'd be on tranquillizers in no time. Assuming I did go to Court, the worst that could happen would be Conway turning round in the Dock, seeing me and thinking harsh thoughts. And, honestly, I didn't give a damn what Conway chose to think.

Besides, there was another little matter filling me with the impulse to go to Court. A very intriguing matter. How, I asked myself, was Warburton going to prove his case? It was on the cards that Conway would plead guilty, in which event the problem would never arise. But just suppose he didn't? And suppose all Warburton had was his own word that the films (Produced, Exhibit numbers 1, 2, and 3) had been in Conway's possession, with the nuns, the nurses or the *au pairs* being shown? Conway would brief a solicitor at taxpayers' expense to explain that it was all a frame-up, that Warburton had planted the evidence and was now telling lies. And with a bit of luck, Conway would come out of it smelling of roses. No, to be in with any sort of chance, Warburton needed a second witness, and even if I'd wanted to — which I didn't any more — I couldn't be it, because I hadn't been there on the night. I'd been watching from a distance, but that would never count.

I wondered if Warburton would have the gall to call Shaun Harker as his witness. Ridiculous, you might think, and ordinarily I'd be inclined to agree with you. But I'd seen so many ridiculous things happen by now that I was virtually beyond surprise. Harker would be entitled to appear and give evidence, just as any witness would, straight or crooked, but whether he'd be bold enough to say he'd been there at the time, taken part in the raid, helped to arrest Conway, these were questions of a much more dubious kind.

Unless Harker turned out to be a lot more than he seemed? Like I just said, there were some screwy things tied up in this job, and wouldn't it be a hell of a lark if young Harker turned out to be a copper in disguise — a sort of special agent on the Dwarf squad who'd been fitted up with a bogus criminal background as part of an official cover story?

Good God, no! Impossible! And yet . . .

But I think I've said enough to explain why I suddenly felt bound to go along to Court and listen to the evidence. I knew the place well enough. The only other thing I needed to know was the date and time of the event. But experience could help me there.

Usually, when people are arrested latish on, they're heaved up before the beak next morning. If not, the alternative is to chuck them out on bail, and somehow I didn't think Conway was a candidate for immediate bail. So it seemed a fair bet that the right time to attend Court was straight away — as soon as the place opened for business. I dragged myself away from Doreen, washed, shaved, donned my wedding and funeral suit and set off.

Parked on the back row of the Public Gallery, I listened to a couple of quick remands and a lot of boring traffic stuff, but I saw no sign of Conway, either in Dock or out. At mid-morning when they had a recess I nipped along to the Press seats and snitched a look at the court sheet. I went through it twice, once skimming and the second time reading more carefully. Conway wasn't listed. I couldn't be sure if that was a conclusive check, or whether they might slip him in as an encore, so I hung about the place till Court finished for the day. He didn't show up.

I had a few kittens when it occurred to me that Conway might be a special case, and they might have had him up before a special court in some other room. But if they'd done that, I was too late. It was over and done with.

I bought two copies of the evening paper — early and late editions — and just about wore the ink off, reading right through to the hatches, matches and despatches. I found two Conways. One was Felicity Conway, aged nineteen, who had a very nice smile and legs all the way up. The other was Neil Simon Conway, born that same day at the General Hospital.

So they had bailed him. They must have done.

Just to be sure, I sweated through the night and got up early to buy a morning paper. No Conways at all. Now I was really worried. I kept telling myself that if they'd bailed him it might be a fortnight before the case came up — and of course that made sound sense — but somehow I couldn't buy that at all. Somehow the whole thing had begun to stink. It was around that stage that I decided to break one of my standing rules. I rang Warburton's number and got an answer right away. But I didn't come right out with what I was after. Hell, no. When you're talking to coppers, you play it nice and soft — and a little bit sneaky.

"I need to have words in your ear, Eric," I told him.

"What about?"

"Not over the phone. It's too delicate altogether. But it's a link-up with you know what."

"Oh hell. You've caught me at a bad time, Peeper. I'm up to my jock-strap in work. Won't it keep for a couple of days?"

"Suit yourself, mate. But this thing could easily go bad on us. It might keep a day. It might fold in a couple of hours."

That line — and its endless variations — has never been known to fail. Within half an hour I was down by the river, climbing into Warburton's car. I must say, he didn't seem pleased to see me — and he might be less pleased when he heard what I had to say — but I didn't give a canary's cock about that.

"What's on your mind, Peeper?" He said for openers.

"Pound notes, for one thing."

"Never mind that. What was this urgent matter you mentioned?"

"I'm a poor man," I lied, "and that's bloody urgent."

"And is that all? Do you mean to tell me you've dragged me all the way out here just to ask for money?"

"I shouldn't have to ask, Eric. The stuff should be ready to hand. If you don't pay, I don't work. And that means tomorrow as well as today. You stand heavily in my debt, young man."

"How do you make that out, for God's sake?"

"Easy. You gave me fifteen quid to

go chasing after your rotten little porn merchant. I spent thirty. So that's fifteen you owe me for starters."

The light of battle burned in Warburton's eyes, but I glared back at him and I knew I was bound to win, because I'd backed the horse both ways. I didn't really care about the few quid involved, but purely on principle I meant to have it — either the money or the other alternative, which I supposed would have suited me better. That alternative was a refusal to pay, leading directly to a break in relations between me and Warburton, and the day I could walk away from this man for ever would be a happy, happy day.

But Warburton knew these things as well as I did. He gave in with manifest reluctance, dragged that fat wallet out again and handed me three blues. I took them and nodded, but I had another card to play yet. I meant to pump him about Conway.

"Thanks, Eric. That straightens us

up. And now, when can I expect a return on the rest of the job?"

"What job?"

Short and sweet. A denial by implication. I didn't like it.

"The Conway job. Good God Almighty, Eric. You don't think I did all that chasing around for nothing?"

He was silent for a minute, and then he surprised me.

"I don't pay out on failures," he said.

Which put me in the sort of situation I've often been in before, where I knew damned well I was being sold a pup of some sort, but didn't want to protest too much till I'd seen its sex, its colour, its size and the number of legs it had. I had to protest a bit, though. I owed it to my conscience.

"Failures? What the hell's that supposed to mean?"

"I mean the bloody thing didn't work out, Peeper. You led me a right merry dance with that one. Mind you, I'm not saying it was your fault, because any job can go sour. But it didn't work. And you can't expect to draw wages if I don't get the goods."

"Look, Eric. You've lost me somewhere along the way. The Conway job was a perfect set-up. It was like shelling peas. You must have had a touch, if you went there at all. Are you telling me you didn't go?"

Warburton gave me what was supposed to be a sad little grin.

"Now don't insult my intelligence, Peeper. I went all right. I put up a resounding black last night. I turned half the Force out to do a drugs raid, and when we got there — nothing. The place was absolutely clean, Peeper."

"No drugs, eh? Well I can understand that, because I told you I wasn't dead sure about drugs. But then there was the dirty pictures. What about the dirty pictures?"

"How many times have I got to say it? The place was clean. No drugs, no films, no people, no nothing. And on the strength of your say-so, I didn't bother getting a warrant, so the bloody man Conway's out for my blood. He's stuck a complaint in already, Peeper. I'll be bloody lucky if he doesn't sue."

7

I KEEP saying, *what the hell was I supposed to do?*, and that's not fair, because I'm the one who's supposed to be telling the story, but I can tell you, I'd have been glad of some good, sound advice about then. Lacking it, I could only rely on my native cunning.

The first thing I had to do was get away from Warburton without giving him any hint that the jig was up. I managed that by switching from anti to pro, expressing my deepest sympathy for the predicament he found himself in, going through the, *I can't understand it at all*, bit, offering to be more careful in future and assuring him that I didn't expect to be paid. I even offered him his fifteen quid back, and if he'd been sharp I might have let him take it, but I'd judged his nature fairly well. He thanked me a bit too profusely for what I'd tried to do, made protestations of good faith and fended the money off. I pocketed the notes, a bit quick, in case he changed his mind.

And we parted on good terms, with mutual promises that we'd have a pint together now and then, and maybe something else would come up that we could get together on. That got me away from Warburton. After that I started to worry like hell about my next move.

The first idea that occurred to me was to forget the whole episode — write it off to experience — and henceforward keep well out of Warburton's way. But that was like saying leave the scorpion crawling over your leg and maybe it'll go away, so I quickly changed my mind. There was something very deep going on, a conspiracy of some sort, and I'd been dragged into it with no chance of saying *no*. And I had no way of knowing whether it was over or just starting; whether I was out of it or due to be dragged back in.

If I'd been able to work out what the thing was about it would have helped some, but either my think-box was addled or the plot was too profound for me. There could be no doubt that Eric Warburton had just fed me a complete cock-and-bull story, and no amount of making allowances or giving the benefit of the doubt could change that. There might well have been no evidence of drugs at Conway's house, but there had been a gathering of people — I'd seen that with my own eyes — and there'd been films too, whether they were Laurel and Hardy films or not. Because I'd seen Warburton with Conway in one hand and the films in the other. You say they might have been empty reel cases? To hell with that. If they had been, he'd never have taken the buggers away.

So it had been lying nonsense to suggest that he found the place clean. And if Warburton had told lies about the things I'd seen, I thought it reasonable that his whole bloody story was false. There had been mucky films on show — maybe drugs as well — and arising from what he'd found there, Warburton had huffed Conway.

But he hadn't charged him, hadn't brought him before the Court. And now he was seeking to deny the whole thing. Why in heaven's name should he bother to do that? To cheat me out of a bit of wage? Not a chance of that. So what, then?

The question was easy. The only answer I could come up with that made any sort of sense was that Warburton and Harker, without having involved any proper policemen, had struck some sort of deal with Conway. They were in alliance, a cop, a crook and a porn and drugs dealer. Alliances don't come any unholier than that.

I made one last despairing attempt to crawl out from under by telling myself it was none of my business, but that didn't work at all. I'm a crook myself, and I'll answer to one or two other unpleasant names that could be thrown at me, but I do have a sort of morality. It's weak and watery, but it's there. My conscience wouldn't let me do nothing. Along with that, I had a more personal angle to contend with. The Conway job was already throwing an ugly black shadow right across my future, and, like the scorpion, ignoring it wouldn't make it go away.

Before my meeting with Warburton in Skinner's caff, only Bert Boggis had known the way I make my living. Warburton had guessed it, but he hadn't known for certain. In retrospect I cursed myself dateless for not having let things stand that way, but I'd bared my soul to Warburton in what I'd accepted as a privileged interview. Now, Warburton knew — and Harker almost certainly knew — and, God help me, that scummy fat Conway probably knew as well. Now that they were in cahoots, Warburton wouldn't hesitate to make the point. I could hear him in my mind's eye, chatting to Harker and Conway over a pint and chortling about the stroke he'd pulled on me.

"You must remember the bloke, Denzil," he'd say. "The one who bought you the pint in the Green Man. The one you invited over to see the show."

"That little swine," Conway would say, also chortling. "I remember him well. I'll mark his bloody card first chance I get."

That, or something like that. And the conversation would take place in front of Conway's cronies. His ugly woman, the boozers, the lechers, the druggies and, for all I knew, Old Uncle Tom Cobley and all.

So it was very much my business — and a bloody sorry business it was too. I might easily be finished in the trade, or worse. But I wasn't going to stand by and let three prime bastards like those make a mess of my life. I was going to fight, and one way or another

I was going to settle their hash in a resounding way.

But how?

What I really needed was help, good solid reliable help, and I wasn't at all sure where I could hope to get it. Not from Doreen. She'd give me sympathy and support, along with all the other things she regularly gave me, and she'd stand by me through the worst of what might come. But it simply wasn't enough. And for similar reasons, Stella couldn't help me either. Stella was a strong and determined woman. She'd stand shoulder to shoulder with me and fight off my adversaries with tooth and claw if need be, but that wasn't the sort of help I needed either. I needed professional help, from somebody who also had the power to act, and I only knew one person in the whole world who could give me that. Bert Boggis himself. Bert would have been ready to give me the answers I needed, if I hadn't been such a flaming fool. Was there a chance he might still help me? I didn't think so. The temptation to run screaming to Boggis, lay my cards on the table and plead for forgiveness, was almost unbearably strong. But I knew I'd let him down badly and I didn't have the guts to face him. Besides, I'd never known him to be in the least sympathetic. So I'd have to live with my sins and trust they didn't find me out. Thinking such morbid thoughts I lost all that evening and most of the following day. I had a flaming row with Doreen, the first for a long time, and nearly finished up without a roof over my head. Offered the chance to make amends in bed, I damned near fumbled that as well, simply because my heart wasn't in it.

Next morning I made my peace with Stella and then spoiled it by swearing at her and smashing a plate in temper. Stella's more easy going than Doreen and I managed to patch things up again (all except the plate) without doing too much real harm, but I knew I wasn't fit company for anybody and I started to have visions of lousing up every relationship I cared anything about. And yet, in a curious way, it was good for me, because I goaded myself and chided myself and finally forced myself into a decision. To hell with all this. I was a ratepayer after all — or Doreen was on my behalf — and it was time I got my money's worth. Never mind friendship and silly things like that. Boggis was a copper, and as everybody knows, coppers are servants of the public, paid by the state.

Bert would blow his top, I didn't have the slightest doubt about that, and he was fully entitled to do just that. But when you came right down to it he was a copper and he lived and breathed his job. So let him hate and despise me as much as he liked, and let him lash me with his tongue if it suited him, but he had a duty to sort out whatever it was that Warburton and company were up to. So to hell with any cash deals, I'd go to Bert as an ordinary member of the public and demand that he do something. *You've got a bent copper*, I'd say. *You've got a porn and drugs ring operating. You've got two bloody rogues linked in with a policeman and they all want catching. So do your duty, Sergeant Boggis.*

And of one thing I could be comfortingly sure — out Boggis would go. He wouldn't stand for what was happening out there. He'd fix Warburton and the rest. And most likely, when it was over, he'd never speak to me again. But it wouldn't matter a damn, because by now I'd resigned myself to it.

★ ★ ★

And would you believe, I'd entirely misjudged the great, lanky, foul-mouthed, sarcastic swine. Oh he had his money's worth out of me, bumping weight, but he didn't ask for any pound of flesh. And after we'd done a lot of sorting out he took me off to a little private club we know of, where it's tolerably safe for us to be seen together, and we both got so stewed that Boggis had to leave his car and we went home in a taxi.

But I'm getting ahead of myself again, and you might be interested in the bits in the middle. Not all of them though, because I don't want to bore you with the bits that were personal to me. So I'll gloss over where he called me some unfriendly names, where he offered to show me the inside of a cell, where he discussed loyalty at some length and where he took my pedigree out with tweezers, dropped it on the floor, ground it with his heel and gave it back to me in ribbons, and I'll move on to the stage where we were sitting together in his office and he knew as much as I did. Please bear in mind, I still wasn't feeling my usual self. Most times I'm as chirpy as a cricket, but I'd had the chirp knocked out of me and I was very subdued.

"You'll have to go through it all again, Peeper," he informed me, his face twitching like a rampant jelly-fish as he displayed all those signs which, in Boggis, pass for merriment.

"Come off it, Bert. I've been through it twice already."

"That was just for my benefit. Now you'll have to do it all again for the benefit of Detective Inspector Atkinson."

"I don't know the bloke. Who is he?"

"You've met him, Peeper. He's Warburton's boss."

"Is he the bloke I met on the Bragg-Norton job?"

"The very same. A nicer bloke you couldn't wish to meet."

"That he may be, but I've no wish to meet him."

"You've got to. There's no way round it, old mate."

"You keep saying that. What I want to know is why?"

"Then I'll tell you. Though I

138

shouldn't have to because we've been through all this before. None of the stuff you've told me about is on my patch. It isn't even in my Force area. And this bastard Detective Constable Warburton isn't under my command. If we manage to get Warburton sacked — and that's what I intend to do without any question, it'll be their Chief Constable, not ours, who'll have to sign the papers. Maybe you're beginning to understand?"

"I still don't see why this Atkinson has to be told."

"Good Lord, Peeper. You're getting old. You were always on the stupid side and you're getting steadily worse. Mr. Atkinson covers the area in question. It's his crime, his blue film show, his drug chain, and Warburton's his man, though I've a feeling he won't be boasting about that after we've talked to him."

"All right, he has to know. But why must I tell him? You know the story. You can pass it on without dragging me into it. Hell-fire, Bert, I've been blown enough, without blowing me to him."

"Nonsense, Peeper. Len Atkinson's the absolute soul of discretion. I've known him since I was a kid. I'd trust him with my life."

"Bugger your life, Bert. This is my life."

"He needs you, Peeper. It's the only way. In any case, he half knows about you already. He paid you out a tidy sum for that silver job, remember, and he's nobody's mug. I kidded him it was just a one-off job, but he has his own views."

So we waited, with the door bolted and an instruction out from Boggis that he wasn't to be disturbed except by the one named visitor. And when Detective Inspector Atkinson arrived I went through everything twice more, just to be sure he got the picture.

* * *

"It's a slowly slowly job, Bert." Atkinson said. "Whatever happens we mustn't jump too early. Between you and me, I've felt dowdy about Warburton for some time. Not for this sort of thing, I hasten to add. But he isn't the best of jacks. He's neglectful. He doesn't turn in a fair day's work."

"Maybe that's because he's working away from home."

"Very probably. And Peeper's story appears to confirm that."

I felt myself warming to this man Atkinson. Frankly, I'd expected a bit of a battle from him and it wouldn't have surprised me greatly if he'd ridiculed the whole story. Hell, it wouldn't have surprised me if he'd turned nasty, locked me up and charged me with blackmail or perjury or whatever. When all was said and done, here was I, a shady character with suspect morals and a well-documented history of crime — and there was Warburton, a cop. Not just a cop, a detective. Not just a detective, but one of D.I. Atkinson's detectives. I couldn't have blamed him if he'd hurled the story back in my face.

In fact, if I faulted the chap at all it was rather from the other direction. I thought maybe he was too understanding, too ready to believe the worst of Warburton. In his position, I felt I'd have supported my own men against an unprepossessing and graceless little snot like me. The fact that he didn't, said something for Atkinson, but whether it said something bad or good I wasn't sure. Maybe it was true that he'd sussed out Warburton in advance of hearing all the dirt from me?

And then again, maybe it was my work in the Bragg-Norton case that had impressed Atkinson in my favour, or maybe it was no more than the influence of Bert Boggis who, in the face of the odds, had put in a good word for me? But it didn't matter a jot either way. Atkinson was on my side. And so, it seemed, was Boggis — more than I had a right to expect.

"If Peeper says it — it's true," Boggis went on, underlining my thoughts. "You've got a bad egg there, I'm afraid."

"I know it, Bert. And I intend to sort him out."

"Can't say I'm too happy with the 'I', sir."

"A figure of speech. What's your objection?"

"I hope you appreciate I want to be in on this job. It's a matter of principle with me. The job's yours, of course, and you call the tune. But I want in, because I have to watch out for Peeper's interest. So I hope we can work together."

"Hand in glove, Bert. It goes without saying."

"Good. I'm glad that's settled. Now how do we tackle it?"

"Very cautiously, till we see the way ahead. The immediate problem is that I don't know enough about the background. This job's been sprung on me rather. I haven't had time to organize."

"Can we take it any further for you?"

"That depends, I'd like a better picture of the *dramatis personae*. This man Conway, for example. I've never come across him before. And I don't know Harker, come to that."

"Harker's one of ours. I've felt his collar a time or two, but Peeper knows him better than I do."

"That's stretching it a bit," I chipped in. "We know each other, and there's no love lost, but I don't know a lot about him."

"Harker's a burglar and an all-round rogue," Boggis explained. "But you might not have tangled with him. From what I hear, he operates mainly on my side of the border."

"And now he's moved over onto my side, Bert."

"Yes. All of a sudden. It's surprising."

Atkinson chuckled.

"No it isn't, Bert. Not really. Because

144

I think I know the reason for it. Young Warburton's the catalyst. I don't doubt he's been palling out with Harker for quite a while. Warburton's a native of this town."

"Funny. I never knew that."

"To be honest, Bert, neither did I till you rang up tonight. But I knew he'd be under discussion, so I grabbed a look at his personal file on the way out. He's one of yours, all right."

"In that case, I wonder why he joined your Force and not ours?"

"I should have thought that went without saying," Atkinson chuckled. "A man has a choice. He chose the best."

"Which is more than can be said for you," Boggis retorted, ending the flurry rather neatly, I thought. Atkinson must have thought so too. He flashed a wide grin.

"*Touché.* I can't quarrel with that. And now, what about Denzil Conway? He's a complete stranger to me."

"And to me," Boggis echoed. "How

about you, Peeper? Can you supply any revealing glimpses?"

"Only what I've told you. Nothing else."

"So he's a case for enquiry, Bert," Atkinson said. "Are these shows of his still going on?" He went on, speaking to me.

"Your guess is as good as mine," I told him. "I haven't been back to check. But they shouldn't be, after a police raid."

"Quite." Atkinson looked suddenly grim. "They should have been chopped for ever. But it wouldn't surprise me in the least to find that they're still going on. And if they are, well, we wouldn't have to argue about what that means."

"I've got a strong stomach," I offered, "and I know the drill for getting in. If you'd like me to do a replay, I'd . . . "

But Boggis was holding up a restraining hand and Atkinson was shaking his head, slowly and expressively.

146

"That won't be necessary, Peeper," Atkinson said. "And what's more important, it could be dangerous. Not only dangerous for you, but damaging to the whole enquiry."

"I don't see why. I was made welcome enough last time, and they're not to know I'm anything but a casual customer who likes the sort of stuff they sell. I'm still well in with Warburton."

"Warburton's the danger man. Assuming he has Conway's ear, and we can't doubt that any more, he'd fluff you straight away. Conway might think little of it but he'd only need to mention it to Warburton and the balloon would burst. Warburton's mind works the same way as ours. He told you to lay off — that the job was closed — and he'd be suspicious as hell if you went again."

I said nothing more. There was sound common sense in what Atkinson said. I was faintly disappointed, because I was warming to the case and it would have suited me to be back in action, but I could see it would have been very bad tactics.

"Listen, gentlemen," Atkinson said. (I smirked, because I'm not often referred to in those terms.) "I reckon we should go slow on this job for the time being. There's nothing really spoiling. If friend Conway is still rolling blue films, that only means a few more nuns raped, and nobody corrupted more than they are already. And as for the drugs, well, it's an on-going thing. Nobody wants to increase the problem, but it'll take no harm for a day or two. Just a few more shots for the same old addicts."

"And what about Warburton?" Boggis wondered. "Does he continue to operate as a jack?"

"I think he must, Bert, for the time being. As things stand, there's a likely offence against discipline and almost certainly a criminal conspiracy of some sort. But you've got to admit, we're a bit low on evidence. As it happens, I believe every word Peeper says, but it's a question of whether the Chief

Constable would believe it — or the Court, if it went that far. The answer in both cases is probably *no*. Or at least, Warburton would have to be given the benefit of the doubt. Besides, I'm sure you wouldn't want to expose your man to that kind of publicity."

"That's true. But I don't like to think of Warburton staying on duty either. It gets under my skin."

"Mine too. And I've no intention of leaving him loose for long. But I still think we should give him a day or two. I could have him suspended, but in the long run that would be a bad thing. He'd know we were after him, and he'd spend the rest of his time covering up and blocking our efforts. No, Bert. When we blast off at Warburton, let's make sure we're loaded in both barrels."

"Agreed. So what next?"

"We've a lot of enquiries to make, you and I. And we'll have to do most of them ourselves, without involving other people, especially other policemen. I

149

think we can break up now, and as for you, Peeper, you can go off and lose yourself for a couple of days. I mean that very definitely. With Warburton and his mates still flying around you're better out of the way. Can you go out of circulation for a couple of days?"

"That's no problem."

"Good. Then that's what you do. But we need to get together again when we've made some progress. What about the day after tomorrow? Shall we say back in this office, about ten a.m.?"

"It's a bad time, sir," Boggis said. "I don't like having Peeper here at all. When he does come, I have to sneak him in and out. You know how it is."

"Fair enough, Bert. Let's choose the same time, but another venue. I think you know where I live?"

"I should do. I've had a whisky or two up there."

"Then come and have some more. You too, Peeper. If you arrange it with Sergeant Boggis you can travel in his car."

* * *

And there I was, separated from the action. They'd done it in a very nice way and I couldn't deny the wisdom of what had been arranged. At the same time I couldn't help feeling a little bit cheated — sort of pushed out. But I consoled myself with the thought that I had very definitely been told to stand by for consultation. I wondered what the chances might be of collecting a consultation fee.

I also took advantage of another, more far-reaching consolation. With all that time on my hands I set to work repairing some of the damage I'd done to my standing with Doreen and with Stella. I travelled to and fro between home (Doreen's place, you'll remember) and the Albion Hotel, like a tennis ball in a long rally, and I spent so much of my time with the ladies that there was a danger of them both getting broody at the same time.

The trouble was, in order to keep

faith with Boggis and Atkinson I couldn't go anywhere else: not to a pub — any pub, because you never could tell when Warburton or Harker — or even Conway — might show up. And particularly not to Vince Skinner's place, because, on his previous track record, Warburton was likely to go looking for me there. In fact, to be absolutely right about it, I shouldn't have been on the streets at all, not even perambulating between two places the way I was. But what the hell! A man's got to live.

All in all, I was very glad when the time came for our appointment. I knew that Boggis and Atkinson had had two days of fun, and I begrudged them that, but at least I was likely to hear the results very shortly.

I might have said that I went to Atkinson's place in style, except that you can't use a word like stylish to describe Bert Boggis's old banger.

8

ATKINSON'S house was very nice; a medium-sized detached house built in that lovely dark cherry-red brick that seems to gleam in all weathers. The front garden was neatly laid out with a mixture of vegetables and flowers. Either he or some member of his family must have green fingers, I thought, unless his budget ran to a gardener. Boggis drove up a longish drive and parked on a big gravel square in front of the house. There would have been room for four or five cars, properly packed in. Poking over a fence at one side I could see the roof of a big greenhouse and on the opposite side there was a big double garage. Atkinson had done very well for himself, I thought. Better than Bert Boggis, whose house was nice enough, but not so grand. But then Atkinson was a detective inspector, and maybe there was a lesson there somewhere.

We were met at the front door by a pleasantly plump lady with greying hair, a pink face and a broad smile. Mrs. Atkinson, I supposed. She showed us through to a side room, where Atkinson waited with a half-filled tumbler in each hand. He gave one to Boggis and one to me, and I settled myself in a big, comfortable chair with enough whisky to make about five doubles. Bert settled too, and he looked nicely at home, but his baggy cord trousers went straight up to half mast and he went through his usual ritual of tugging at them to try to cover his shanks. I couldn't help wondering what his superior officer thought about Bert's turn-out, but judging from his face he never even noticed.

And we weren't there to discuss clothes. Not counting the greetings all round, I was the first to be spoken to.

"Let's start by putting you in touch, Peeper," Atkinson said. "Sergeant Boggis and I have a few things to talk about still, but most of it we both know, so I'll brief you on the rest. The whole thing's a bit touchy, by the way. I'm going to be talking about things that I wouldn't like to have spread about, but Sergeant Boggis tells me we can trust you. Isn't that so, Bert?"

"Tell him to shut his mouth, it stays shut."

"Very well then. So we're talking in confidence. I think the first thing to tell you is that my enquiries serve to back up your story as far as it goes, but in a negative way. I checked up on Warburton's duties for three nights ago, when you tell me he arrested Conway. Each officer has to fill in a page of his duty diary for every working day, showing the duties he was engaged in. Warburton's entry for that night is very skimpy indeed, not that that surprises me, because he always has kept poor records. The point is, he showed himself as being on general enquiries at public houses, with no specific cases in mind, and he booked off at ten-thirty. What time do you say he arrested Conway?"

"I don't know the exact time, but it was well after that. I didn't go there myself till closing time and I must have waited half an hour or so. Allowing for walking time, I'd say it was about half past eleven."

"That's point number one, then. When he arrested Conway he'd been officially off duty for something like an hour. It isn't all that important, by the way. It isn't unknown for a detective, quite properly, to book himself off duty and then come upon some incident that makes it necessary to book back on again. If that happened, according to the rules he'd make an extra entry in the diary, a supplementary. There's no supplementary entry in Warburton's diary."

Atkinson paused, picked up the whisky bottle and came to offer a refill. I covered my glass up quick. Lordy, I might be a seasoned drinker, but I couldn't shift whisky that quick. Boggis took another smidgen, but I think he was just being polite.

"So I moved on from the man's own record," Atkinson went on, "and did a check of the office records. I didn't expect to find anything and that's exactly what I found. Nothing. No arrest sheet, no charge form, not even an entry in the 'Visits to Police Stations' book. Now I'd better explain, as I told you earlier, Bert, that I couldn't go round questioning the staff. That's the devil of a case involving a police officer. It isn't a question of loyalty or trust. I can trust most of the station staff to be honest and decent, but I can't trust them not to whisper amongst themselves. They gossip like old women, and sooner or later the word gets out and the damage is done. So I didn't ask questions generally, but I did have a long session with the Chief Inspector in charge of the shift — who happens to be fully reliable — and it turned out he didn't know a damned thing about any enquiry involving drugs, blue films or anything like that. And the point is, he certainly would have heard about it, if Warburton had done anything officially. So I think we can safely say that anything he did that night was off his own bat. I can take that a little bit further. Anything he did that night was highly unofficial and almost certainly against the interests of the Force."

"A singularly undesirable officer," Boggis commented.

"You can say that again, Bert, with knobs on. And now I'll tell you how undesirable he is. I dug up some information yesterday that would have disbarred him from joining the Force if we'd known about it at the time. He comes from a criminal family. He has two brothers, both of whom have served time for burglary."

"Hell's bells." Boggis looked genuinely shocked. "But if that's so, your recruiting department must have dropped a real clanger."

"They did, Bert, and in another sense they didn't. The trouble seems to be that our vetting procedure — and yours too, I suspect — isn't geared to cope with peculiar situations, unless those situations are brought directly to the department's notice."

"Go on. I'm interested in peculiarities."

"Different names, Bert. That's the short answer. And a completely different district to boot. Warburton's brothers were born out of wedlock and the births were registered in the mother's maiden name. Later on she married their father and went on to produce Eric Warburton. But because she'd married the man Warburton by then, she registered the third child in her husband's name."

"I've heard of similar cases," Boggis said, "but I still can't understand how those details slipped through. He'd have to supply the names of referees. Wouldn't the referees have given the game away?"

"You'd think so, but they didn't.

159

And to the best of my knowledge they were perfectly respectable people. The answer seems to be that they didn't know about Mrs. Warburton's other two sons, and you'll see why, when I tell you the rest of the story."

"I'm all ears."

"Well then. The first two lads were born in London, and because their mother was a single parent, her mother, the kids' grandmother, took charge of their upbringing. Later on, their father got the offer of a job in this district, so he married the mother and moved out. By that time, the other two lads had settled in with their grandmother and it was decided they should stay there. That meant that Eric Warburton, born up here, was raised as an only child."

I'd taken a bit of a back seat by this time, mainly because I was fascinated with this little story and didn't wish to interrupt. I could see that Bert Boggis was fascinated too, but he wasn't content to sit and listen.

"I can see how it could happen," he

said. "But what I'd like to know is how the hell you found out about it after all this time."

"A trade secret, Bert. No, I'm only joking. I don't mind telling you. One of our old retired sergeants lives a few doors away from Warburton. It's on your patch, just. He's a bachelor, and since he retired he's taken to chatting-up Mrs. Warburton over the garden gate. Old Man Warburton died a few years ago it seems, but I don't think there's anything hatching between these two — it's just a bit of neighbourly friendship. Anyway, they're well past the confidence stage and over the years she's slipped him a few of her secrets, including that one. I called in on the old man yesterday, only because I was passing and remembered him, and before you know it, he'd passed me the word, all innocent like."

"He told you they were crooks?"

"Hell, no. I don't believe he knows about that. And if he'd known, I don't suppose he'd have mentioned it at all.

But you're an old copper, just as I am. If you'd picked that information up about somebody you were interested in, what would you have done?"

"Checked up at the Yard."

"And that's exactly what I did. They've got quite a bit of form, though they've been quiet recently, and there's nothing to suggest they've ever operated outside the London area. I've asked for copies of their records though, because you never know."

"And I suppose if Warburton had declared these unsavoury siblings he'd have been turned down for the job?"

"We wouldn't have been keen on taking him, that's for sure. Even though he has no contact with his brothers as far as we know. We'd have thought it risky to employ him. And now, by God, we know it would have been."

Atkinson paused again and nodded at my glass. I shook my head.

"Well, Bert. That's about all I have to report. So for Peeper's benefit, I suggest you give us the bits you have."

"I've been chasing up Harker and Conway," Boggis said. "In relation to Harker, I've nothing to report that you don't know about already. It isn't Harker's pedigree we're after, it's his collar in our hands with some evidence to hold it there. Conway, now, he's a bit of a mystery man. Trying to find out about him has been difficult, mainly because I was in the same boat as you — I couldn't go round openly, asking questions. I took a chance early on last night and called in for a pint at the Green Man. It's a hell hole, as you probably know, and I don't ever want to go there again except on business. Working on Peeper's description, I'd have recognized Conway if he'd been there, but he wasn't there. So I downed a pint in a very unfriendly atmosphere and walked out.

"But I did see Conway, later on, and there's no mistaking him. As we agreed, I kept obboes on his house. I used the same place you did, Peeper, and it's very good, though I could have done with a pair of wellington boots. Anyway, the net result of standing there for a couple of hours is that I can tell you the show still goes on. I watched the buggers rolling up in droves with Conway in the lead. If I was short of confirmation before, that Warburton's bent, that was enough to convince me. Conway hadn't a care in the world. He certainly wasn't afraid of any police raid, and that, of course is Warburton's doing. It annoyed me to see the clans gathering. I damned near went in and broke it up."

"You didn't, though, as I know."

"Hell, no. I can control my feelings. But I'm not as far forward with Conway as I'd like to be. After the show had started I wandered up and down the street for a while, hoping to find one of his neighbours hanging around, maybe somebody with a grudge against Conway. If I'd found anybody, I'd have chatted them up, casually. But there was nobody around, and I didn't think it wise to go knocking on doors."

"So we still don't know much about Conway, apart from this little private industry of his? We don't know if he's a family man, where he hails from or what he does for a living?"

"No, we don't. And it would be nice if we could find out. But if we dig too deep, we'll alert him, and through him, Warburton. Mind you, I think we've played about too long with this one. I vote we lay on another raid, and let it be a proper one this time."

"I'm almost at that stage myself," Atkinson said, "but I'm going to let it run at least another day. I've got some late news, Bert, that even you don't know. I've dug up an old contact in that area, a good informer for me, in his day. He knows the Green Man, goes in there sometimes, and I've fixed it with him to go there tonight and feel around. He's a good man, and with the grounding he's already got I think he might manage to find something out."

"It's worth giving him a chance, anyway."

"That's what I think, Bert. So we'll hold back on the Conway job till at least tomorrow. I'll keep in touch with my man. If he takes us any further, we'll have a confab. If not, we'll hit Conway tomorrow, and hit him hard."

★ ★ ★

There was no invitation to me to join in the proceedings and I didn't expect one. But I was more than pleased with the way things had gone. My part in the Conway case was definitely and finally over, and all I had left was the confidence that the job would be done properly this time. After the experiences I'd had with Eric Warburton I was more than satisfied with that confidence.

★ ★ ★

With the rest of the day to kill, I had an hour with Stella and then went home. It isn't often I stay in the house all afternoon and evening, but I almost managed it this time. There was nothing much on telly though, and by nine o'clock I was suffering from a parched throat and itchy feet. Neither Boggis nor Atkinson had said anything more about lying low, and I couldn't see any harm in trotting to the local for the last hour, so I did another thing I don't do as often as I should. I offered to take Doreen out for a drink — and she jumped at the chance. It didn't take her long to doll herself up. She looked pretty enough to eat, and we set off in high spirits.

We walked arm-in-arm, heading for the nearest pub, and a couple of minutes stroll brought us in sight of Vince Skinner's caff. The idea was to go straight on by, but we never got that far, because there were two motor bikes parked on the pavement outside the caff. I'm not the world's best at motor bike recognition but there was something very familiar about them, and when I looked at the number plates I could have sworn one of them was Shaun Harker's bike. But I couldn't be absolutely sure, and although I remembered having written the number down I couldn't check it, because I don't keep empty cigar packets and I'd jettisoned that one some time ago.

I stopped in my tracks, nearly wrenching Doreen's arm off in the process. Not surprisingly, she put in a request for an explanation.

"What do you think you're playing at, you silly man?"

I was slow answering, because I had to make my mind up what my answer ought to be. I came to a decision pretty quick.

"I want you to do a little job for me, Doreen."

"Such as what?"

"Such as to go into Vince Skinner's caff and buy a coffee."

"But I don't want a coffee."

"You can gulp it down. Or you can

leave it on the counter for all I care. The coffee's just an excuse for going in there."

"What do I need an excuse for?"

So I told her. I didn't tell her why I needed the information and I knew she'd never guess. (One of these days I've really got to give Doreen a full explanation and then maybe she'll understand about a lot of things.) I told her to go in, locate the two motor bike men, memorize their descriptions and then come back out and report to me. Doreen's a good girl. She went off without a murmur.

I waited about five minutes and there she was again.

"Did you manage to sort them out?" I asked her.

"I couldn't miss, could I? They're the only two in there."

"Tell me what they look like."

"Well, one of them is young Shaun Harker, if that helps."

Oh boy, did that help. But I didn't let on. I kept a straight face and cocked my head to one side, simulating thought.

"Harker. Harker. Is that somebody I should know?"

"Of course you know him. The big rough young lad who lives up Seville Street. You know. The one who set fire to the school."

"Oh, that lad. So that's Harker, is it? I wonder where he got the loot to buy a bike like that? What does the other look like?"

She gave me a damned good description of Warburton, there was no mistaking it. And at the same time she ruined any chance she might have had of a nice quiet drink with me.

"You'll have to go back home, love," I told her.

I won't bore you with the rest of the conversation. It meant that ten minutes after we'd left the house, Doreen was on her way home again, a very disgruntled lady. She was good and mad, and she left me on the understanding (to be revoked at some early date, I fervently hoped) that I should never show my face at her house again. It was our very worst quarrel. I'll go so far as to say that if we'd have been married she'd have been shouting for a divorce.

After Doreen had gone, I took up sentry-go in a dark doorway across the street, almost opposite the front of the caff. I hadn't the slightest idea why I did it, except that it seemed a reasonable thing to do. I would have put plenty of money on, at short odds, that my two disreputable mates were in there for a cup of coffee, no more. If that was all, my time would be entirely wasted. But they were the quarry, and even though they were most likely engaged in a harmless pursuit they were still worth keeping an eye on. It occurred to me quite early, that I was ill-equipped. If they came out, mounted their steeds and roared away there wasn't a blind thing I could do to stop them. But it pleased me to hope that they might do something stupid that would justify all my hanging about.

I'd been there about twenty minutes, and I was beginning to regret my foolish impetuosity, when a small dark van rolled up and parked opposite the caff, on my side of the road but a few car lengths further along. I ignored it, because it didn't mean a damned thing to me. A man climbed out of the van, walked across the road and went into the caff. I ignored him as well, for the same reason, until he was passing in through the lighted door. And then I noticed he was wearing a dark blue uniform and a flat peaked cap.

I was interested, but not all that much, and I used the bloke to relieve my boredom. I dreamed up a fantasy that maybe he was a cop, and for want of something better to think about I asked myself if he might be another bent copper. Maybe the police force was full of the sods? Maybe they were breeding? Maybe Eric Warburton had roped in one of his uniformed mates to help out with whatever his scheme was?

So I took a closer look at the van, and in the glow from a street lamp I could see the word SECURITY painted across the van's rear doors. I strolled over for a closer look still. It had the same word painted along both sides. It occurred to me that whichever security firm owned the van they were well hooked on the power of advertising. And having given birth to that trite thought, I damned near walked away and forgot about it. But there was some more writing on the van, a name and address painted in smaller lettering on the nearside door. I read it in the same way as you read bus tickets or cans of Harpic in the bog.

BRAGG-NORTON CHROME
AND METAL CO.
LONG CANTON TRADING ESTATE,
MORTLEY.

A local van. A familiar name. But I hadn't realized they ran their own security. Well, it explained why the driver wore uniform, and fairly obviously he'd nipped off the night shift to grab a quick cuppa and a pasty. Funny though, that . . .

HELL'S BELLS AND BUCKETS OF BLOOD!!

Even then, I chided myself for having a bad mind. I really would have to stop seeing devils and hobgoblins all over the place. It was getting so that decent people couldn't pass me by without rousing suspicions. Maybe I was becoming obsessed with crime? But there was no getting away from it, it was a hell of a coincidence that a van from the firm who owned the silver, the snout who turned the job in and the detective who'd handled the recovery should all three come together again in these circumstances. Wasn't it possible the bloke had come to see Warburton. No. He couldn't have.

But he might have — and they might be cooking something up right this minute, behind the steamy windows of Skinner's caff. Right or wrong, I had to have a peek in there somehow, and I daren't go inside or Warburton and Harker would recognize me straight off. I did a bunny hop across the street and strolled the full length of the caff frontage, having a good look while pretending to pass by. I couldn't see a bloody thing. I could see in through the windows and I could see most of the tables, but the ones on view were empty. That was where knowing the place helped me. There were two tables tucked in round the corner, out of view from the front windows, and Warburton and Co must be sitting at one of them. The snag was, how was I going to make sure?

I wished like mad I hadn't sent Doreen packing. I even considered digging her out again and sending her in for another coffee, but it would take me at least half an hour to persuade her to speak to me, and in that time — in a tenth of that time — they might have split up and gone.

There's a little entry running up the side of Skinner's place and it leads through to the back street. I nipped up the entry and tiptoed along till I came to the gate leading into his back yard. It was locked, but I shinned over. I knocked the lid off a dustbin and it fell with a clatter, but I held my breath for a minute and nobody came flying out, so I guessed nobody had heard. I felt a bit uneasy, standing in Skinner's yard. All I needed now was a patrolling constable to come along, shine his torch over the gate and start burbling about being on enclosed premises for an unlawful purpose. But that was a chance I had to take. I moved across the yard, slowly and carefully, till I came to the end window. I didn't know for sure whether I could be seen by anybody glancing out, but I kept low just in case. I cocked my eye round the curtain and peeped in.

Well, I'd guessed right anyway. They were sitting at a table in the far corner — all three of them. Their heads were bent in what seemed to be earnest conversation. So I'd established the contact, but I hadn't begun to establish a reason for it. There might be all sorts of explanations for the meeting, hardly any of them sinister. Maybe it was no more than casual — a gregarious customer not liking to sit on his own. The chap in the thick blue serge might be Harker's uncle — or Warburton's — who happened by chance to be on the security staff at the Bragg-Norton place. Or maybe one of them was courting his daughter? Or he could be a fellow motor bike enthusiast, or maybe just a next door neighbour who happened by chance . . . But I couldn't help feeling that none of this had happened by chance, and as I went on eavesdropping on the little cameo I saw something that seemed to confirm my feeling.

Daft as it seemed, Warburton suddenly ducked into my view. What I mean is, he deliberately moved his upper body slightly towards me, so that I could see him better. At the same time he fixed his eyes on something away to my far right. The only thing I could think of that lay in that direction was the counter — and of course fat old Vince Skinner, the proprietor. Warburton was really ducking out of Vince's view and only giving me a better sight of him by accident, but his movement was revealing in more ways than one.

I saw him lower his forearm to the table top and leave it lying there, open palm uppermost, for all the world as though he were asking for money. The security bloke, who was facing Warburton with his back half turned to me, dipped a hand into his pocket, brought something out and slid it over into Warburton's palm. So the bugger was taking bribes now. Was there no end to his wickedness? But if it was a bribe it was in kind rather than cash. I saw a brief gleam and realized it must be silver; but if it was one of those ingots it was a damaged one. A whole corner had been chopped out of it. The thing was only there for a second, and then Warburton drew his arm back and pocketed it.

And I didn't think it was silver,

either. I thought it was a gun — one of those little flat automatic pistols with a snub nose. I was trying to work out the implications of that, when the security bloke took his cap off, threw his head back and roared with laughter. As an academic point I'll say that I could hear the laughter good and strong, but I wasn't listening so much as looking. Because that was when I got my first look at the man's face, and it shook me so much I forgot all about the gun.

Denzil Conway.

We learn chiefly by experience, and I'd just learned more about Conway than Boggis had been able to find out. I knew his occupation. I knew the firm he worked for. And in the same instant a lot of missing bits of the picture fell into place. When I started to add the points up, I knew I had to contact Boggis without delay.

I'd often made the point to Bert Boggis — jokingly, of course — that he ought to supply me with one of those handy little pocket radios, so that if I needed to raise him quickly I could just press the button and get on with it. What a godsend that would have been right now. I knew there was a telephone in the back room of the caff, and I briefly entertained the notion of kicking Skinner's back door in and grabbing the phone. But it was just one of those wild, hopeless thoughts that we all get sometimes. The nearest kiosk was two streets away, and if I shot off to ring Bert I could easily miss some other important detail. And if I didn't go and ring him, I might lose the value of the information I already had. So I was faced with a real problem.

It didn't last long. I hardly had time to toss a mental coin before I heard their chairs scraping and all three got up to go. The party was over, but it might go on longer in another place.

I nipped back across the yard, dragged myself to the top of the gate, checked that the back street was clear and rolled over. I lost a minute creeping round to the front, and when I reached the corner and poked my nose round, Harker and Warburton were straddling their motor bikes ready to kick off, and Conway was waddling across the street towards his van.

They went off in procession — Conway the General, the Lord Mayor or the Visiting Royalty, Warburton and Harker the escort of outriders — and I could only stand there and watch them go.

★ ★ ★

I cursed Bert Boggis long and soundly under my breath. I'd used three coins already and I didn't have an endless supply. I'd tried his extension at the nick and got a big round *no reply*. I'd rung the switchboard again and asked them for his whereabouts; something Boggis had told me never to do except in dire emergency, but hell, this emergency was as dire as anything. I'd even rung the nick at Mortley and asked for Detective Inspector Atkinson, but that useless bugger was missing as well. People kept asking me if I wished to leave a message, but what sort of message could I leave that would alert Boggis or Atkinson without alerting the rest of the world?

When I was desperate enough, I mulled over the idea of asking to speak to another detective — any detective — but I shied away from that one. I knew Warburton was out of the way, but suppose there were other dormant, potential Warburtons? I couldn't be sure about that, and it was a risk I couldn't take.

So I tried to ring Boggis at his home. He wasn't in — of course he wasn't. He seldom is — but his wife answered. Now there is an ill-matched couple, if you like. Jenny Boggis is a hell of a nice person, nice-natured, pretty and sensible. I still can't believe that she ever saw enough in her ragbag of a husband to want to marry him and bear his children, but I've long since stopped trying to rationalize this curious circumstance. I've never actually met her — by deliberate avoidance on Bert's instructions — but she's a real looker, because I've seen her once or twice from a distance. I never give Jenny my name when I ring up, but she knows my voice well enough, and I have sexual fantasies listening to hers.

"I'm expecting him in any time," she assured me, but I knew that was about as certain as picking the winner of the Grand National.

"I need him, Jenny. I really do need him."

"Well, I'll try to raise him if I can, but you know I can't promise. If it's urgent, maybe you could give me an outline?"

It was tempting, but I gave her a *no thanks*. I'm under strict orders from Boggis, never to involve Jenny beyond leaving a contact message, and I know there are damned good reasons for that.

"If he comes in, where can he contact you?"

That question gave me pause too, because if I gave the number of the kiosk I'd have to hang about there, waiting, and maybe I could employ myself better on the move. But where the hell could I possibly start. Reluctantly, I decided to wait. I gave the number.

"Tell him to ring and keep ringing," I said. "And if you can think of any way of contacting him, I wish you would."

★ ★ ★

And that was that, for the moment. The world had stopped and was screaming for a shove to get going again. While I was hanging about waiting for a call that might never come, I started to get my usual dose of cold feet. Suppose there really was very little in what I'd seen? All right, the gun seemed to put a serious slant on the case. But did it make it urgent? Maybe Conway and Warburton and Harker had gone off happily to bed to be up early next morning and go off starting races? Maybe I was getting all worked up for nothing? Maybe the only person worrying about anything was me. And yet I felt impelled to get my message through somehow. If it proved a false alarm there would be no harm done, except that Boggis would bend my ear about it for a fortnight. But if I'd come upon something very wrong, and I neglected to do anything about it, he'd murder me.

9

TALK about perseverance. I loitered about in that wretched street, counting the bricks in house walls and the cracks in the pavement, for more than an hour. All the time I was blowing hot and cold about whether to stick it or not and I gave it another five minutes at least half a dozen times.

I heard the Town Hall clock give me midnight in slow, booming strokes. I wondered how folk living nearby managed to put up with that din, every hour on the hour, and then I remembered that Doreen's house wasn't all that far away, and the chimes never seemed to bother me. Did they bother Doreen? I'd have to ask her.

Doreen! I was on a bit of a sticky wicket there. I was a long way from being her favourite man. And this wasn't the first time I'd upset her through trying to do the right thing, not by many a dozen. All those other times I'd managed to repair the damage, and maybe I could this time. I hoped so, because I've got very strong feelings for that woman. But you might say my little spat with Doreen helped me along in a perverse way. If it had never happened; if I'd been free to toddle off home and nestle up in my little nest; I'd have jacked this silly job in, long before now. And in any event, I wasn't going to put up with it much longer. It was down to Boggis and all his colleagues to worry about law and order, not to me. I only wanted the jobs that paid wages, and this one was well outside that category. And yet, I honestly didn't want to jack it in. Not till I'd passed the word on to Boggis anyway. If only the silly sod would ring up.

Jenny Boggis would have done her best for me, I knew that, but it was plain she'd failed to raise Bert. And by this time she'd have given up and gone to bed. Or would she? Maybe I'd really impressed her with the urgency of the job, and maybe she was still trying? I made my mind up to call the whole thing off, but before I cleared off it seemed only fair to ring Jenny and tell her, so she could forget about it too.

I got my coin out, stepped into the kiosk and reached out for the phone. And at that minute the bloody thing rang. It was Boggis, and he sounded a bit narked, but narked or not, he sounded good. For once in a while I was pleased to hear his voice.

"What is it, Peeper? And won't it keep?"

I started to tell him. I've mentioned before how quickly Boggis can change his tune. He snapped a few monosyllables in response to the first general outline, but his voice softened an awful lot when I started to enlarge, and by the time I'd finished he'd forgotten all about going to bed and he even sounded civilized.

"Where are you now?"

I told him.

"Hang on there," he instructed. "I'll have to fix a few things up and then nip out and collect you."

It was another twenty minutes, but waiting was a good deal easier this time. And the delay didn't mean Boggis was taking things easy, because when he arrived he was in a steaming hurry. He did a sort of rolling half-stop, with one hand on the wheel and the other holding the passenger door, and he was off again before I could get the door shut after me. He didn't say anything at all — not *hello* or *kiss my arse*. He just put his foot to the boards and we screamed along the main street like it was Brands Hatch. I don't mind going fast when I'm driving, but I was less happy with that crazy Bert Boggis at the wheel.

"You want to watch it, mate," I warned him. "The coppers are all bastards in these parts. You want to get your foot off . . . "

"You want to keep your mouth shut,

Peeper. I'm in a hurry."

"Whereabouts are you aiming to pile the car up?"

If he heard me he didn't let on, so I tried again.

"I object to being kidnapped. I demand to be released. Now tell me where we're going, Bert, or stop the bloody car."

"You'll find out soon enough. Now cut the cackle."

I could see that Boggis was in no mood for banter, so I gave up. He tore over the level crossing and out through the town boundary, and as soon as we hit the street lights of Mortley I knew damned well where we were going. Bert must have guessed my jealousy of Harker. He was taking me with him on an actual job, the decent old sod.

The Bragg-Norton factory is quite a complex in its own right and if a place the size of a city block can be said to be isolated, it's isolated. Bragg-Norton were first to build on a strip of open land on the far side of Mortley, and apart from partly built factories the nearest buildings are on a council estate clustered round the main road. We went through the council houses in something like ten seconds and it wasn't till we turned off on the factory road — which is a big wide strip but in need of some pot-hole filling — that he slowed down to about fifty. I was happier then. Tarmac makes for a smooth ride, but with Bert Boggis at the wheel, bumps and lurches are a damned sight safer than tarmac.

Looking ahead, I could see signs of unusual activity around the factory. Three or four police cars with their blue lights flashing were parked in a heap around the main gate, and an assortment of bods — most of them in uniform — were milling around in the same area. A uniformed copper signalled us to stop, but Boggis ignored him and kept rolling. As we went past him, the copper threw up a very smart

191

salute, having entirely miscalculated the rank of the officious sod who wouldn't stop for a policeman's signal.

Detective Inspector Atkinson was waiting near the gate. He ran across to the car as we drew up. Boggis wound his window down and Atkinson stuck his head in.

"We were too late, Bert. Missed the buggers by half an hour."

"Damn! What's the strength of it?"

"One dead. One shot in the arm, two others tied up. That's all the night security staff."

"The bastards. I didn't bank on that."

"Nor I. But that's what we've got. I've sent for the big brass. I'm going to be tied up here for some time and I'm going to need a good second man, so if you like, you can chuck your weight in under the Force Liaison and Old Pals Act."

"Have we any leads? Any descriptions?"

"Three masked men, that's all. The old nylon stocking trick. So nobody

192

knows who they were for sure. But I think we do, don't we, Bert. And I'm glad to say, thanks to Peeper here, that I've been able to chuck one in the cells."

"Which one?"

"Conway. We found him trussed up in his office, and the first thing he gave us was the old story about how he'd been set upon by ruffians and how they'd overcome him in spite of his spirited resistance." Atkinson chuckled. "I reckon he could have used clean underpants when I told my lads to put the cuffs on him."

"Is he talking?"

"What do you think? No, Bert, he's hollering for solicitors and demanding his rights, but he can do all the hollering he wants."

"No sign of Warburton or Harker then?"

"Nothing. They got clean away. And maybe that's where you come in. I've put out a call to have them brought in, and I want their drums searching.

I thought you could lead one of the teams."

"I brought Peeper along," Boggis said, a bit lamely I thought. "You'll probably want to talk to him."

"I do, but that can wait. I need to talk to you first, Bert. Privately, if you don't mind. So let's take a walk."

Boggis climbed out of his car and slammed the door. Atkinson stuck his head back in and gave me a friendly nod.

"You stay where you are, Peeper," he said. "Don't talk to anybody about anything. If any of my lads start quizzing you, tell them Inspector Atkinson says to go and get stuffed."

And they were gone, leaving me with some pretty harrowing things to think about. Murder, for starters. Neither of them had used that term, but it was the right term if I hadn't misheard Atkinson. I don't like guns, in fact I hate the nasty things, and I could still see that little shiny object Conway had passed to Warburton two or three

194

hours ago. *Two or three hours*. It was actually about two and a half hours, I calculated, and in the intervening time the blasted thing had been used to kill one man and injure another. And Conway had laughed when he'd passed it over, as though he didn't give a damn how many it killed.

But I can tell you, I gave a damn. I gave a lot of damns. I couldn't rid myself of the sick, guilty feeling that if I'd taken some action earlier I might have prevented this happening. If I'd rushed in and grabbed the gun . . . ? But no, I couldn't blame myself for that. It would hever have worked, and I might have finished up on the mortuary slab myself. But if I hadn't wasted so much time trying to pass the word; if I'd traced Boggis sooner; if I'd . . . ? Oh hell, what was the use? I'd done my best, hadn't I? And yet, maybe I could have done better. Maybe if I'd just said *to hell with Boggis*, and made an ordinary citizen's report to the nick; maybe then the poor dead sod in yonder would still be alive?

I don't know why I always have to scourge myself this way, but it happens all the time. I'm not an honest man by any means and no concept of morality ever stopped me lining my pockets. But I draw the line at some things, especially a thing like this. I'd never been much taken with either Warburton or Harker, but they'd turned out to be blacker-hearted bastards than I'd ever credited them with being. It hurt me badly to think this way. I tried to push the thoughts out of my mind.

I didn't have to be rude to any policemen, because none came. I just had to put up with another spell of waiting. But it was nice and comfortable in the car, and while I couldn't make much of what was going on around me, at least there was something to watch and it made the time pass quickly. When Atkinson and Boggis came back they both climbed into the car, Boggis in front, Atkinson behind, and they sat there looking at me in a strange way. I got the impression they were crowding me; making use of the psychological advantage of a two-to-one situation. The crafty buggers had something in mind, but they wouldn't find me an easy victim. It was Atkinson who kicked off — pulling rank, I supposed.

"I've got a very serious proposition to put to you, Peeper," he said. "I've had a word with Sergeant Boggis and he agrees with what I have in mind. The question now is whether you agree."

"What's the proposition?" I asked guardedly.

"We want you to attend court and give evidence."

I told him in salty terms to leave this place and have fun elsewhere in solitude. It was rude of me, but it struck the right note to convey my feelings. Boggis didn't approve. His head shook and I could hear him quietly tut-tutting. Then he said:

"I'm surprised at you, Peeper. We

can manage without gutter language between friends. Now stop being so hasty. Listen to what the man has to say before you fly off the handle."

"I don't have to listen. The answer's no."

"Why not, for heaven's sake?"

"Come off it, Bert. You know damned well why not."

"I know the usual reasons, Peeper. But this is a special case. Mr. Atkinson needs a witness. He's got a murder on his hands and he knows bloody well who did it, but he doesn't have the evidence to prove it. He wants you as a witness."

"Never mind what he wants," I said, deliberately snubbing Atkinson. "What do you want, Bert? I'd like to have your honest opinion on this. Do you think I should give evidence?"

"Yes, Peeper. I do."

I gave him a look of utter contempt. If they could see my face it must have been quite a picture. I simply couldn't believe that this was Boggis talking. He seemed to be suggesting, in cold blood, that I should commit professional suicide by standing up in some wretched court room and admitting that I was a police informer. We'd discussed this very point many times and we'd always agreed there was no way it could ever happen. It didn't matter what the case was or how important, he'd always insisted till now. No case was so important that he'd risk exposing me. I'd fallen for it all the way, and now he was going back on his own principles.

"Don't talk so flaming stupid, Bert," I told him. "If I give evidence I'll be blown for ever. There'd be nothing left for me but to up sticks and emigrate. Is that what you want?"

"It might not come to that," Boggis said. "We'll try to stitch these buggers up another way, and if we can, you won't have to appear at all. I hope to God we can keep you out of it, if you want my honest opinion, but Mr. Atkinson needs to have some positive evidence up his sleeve in case all else fails."

"And if all else fails, you'll sell me down the river?"

He winced. I could see I'd hurt him, but I didn't care.

"I wouldn't call it that," he said, "but yes, if you want to call it dirty names. We've got a real problem here, Peeper, and it's got to be solved. If that means we have to shove you in the box, well, old mate, that's what I'm asking you to do."

Game, set and match to Boggis. I couldn't hold out against that sort of appeal. And although I'd never dream of telling him so, the proposition didn't bother me a lot. Given the choice, I'd rather not have involved myself, but if the alternative was that Warburton and his mates might beat the rap and go on their way rejoicing, well, I didn't have that choice.

"And what exactly will I be expected to say?"

"Everything you can. About Warburton

approaching you; the set up at Conway's house and at the Green Man; the supposed raid by Warburton and the supposed arrest of Conway. The gun incident of course, that's most important, and then the silver."

"What silver? Come off it, Bert, you've got to be joking. That was a straight up job. The silver went back months ago."

"And now it's gone again."

"The whole batch of it?"

At this stage, Atkinson nosed back into the conversation.

"No. That's not true, Peeper. It's the same batch about five times over. Something like fifty thousand quids worth of the stuff. You didn't think Warburton was settling a grudge, did you? He was here for profit, and the poor bugger in yonder got in his way."

★ ★ ★

And somehow, I found myself watching Conway's house again. Bert made the point that if I was going to be a witness I might as well stay with the game. He wouldn't let me inside, but I sat in his battered black Consul parked in the street and watched the event take place. It was different from the previous effort in several ways. The street was full of cop cars making no attempt to be unobtrusive. Half a dozen stalwart lads in blue stood guard at the front and I knew another bunch had gone round the back. Most of the nearby houses had lights in their windows and people in dressing-gowns were creeping down their garden paths to find out what the fuss was about. There was no crowd of visitors at the house itself — they'd hardly be running dirty pictures at that hour — but Conway himself was there, handcuffed to a uniformed bobby, and I didn't suppose he was relishing the prospect of coming home. And it was a proper raid this time, an adequate team for the job. Conway was pushed in front, with Boggis and a bunch of local jacks following close behind.

I suppose it took them twenty minutes to complete the task, though it seemed longer. I saw Conway brought out, still handcuffed, and taken into the back of a police van. Then the officers came out, loaded with projector and screen and rolls of film, as well as various other parcels that I couldn't identify. There'd be no problems about evidence if I was any judge.

Boggis was last to appear, and by that time the street was clearing fast. I expected him to be pretty chuffed, but far from it. He had a face like a wad of torn-up lottery tickets. He climbed in and sat back in his seat. He groaned.

"Success?" I enquired hopefully.

"Success be damned. That was an abject bloody failure."

"How come? They seemed to get the films all right."

"Stop being stupid, Peeper," he said unkindly. "What the hell do I care about a few mucky films? That's just flea-bite stuff — a bike without lights.

We got some drugs as well, and that's better than nothing, I suppose. But no silver. I wanted silver. Let's hope the other lads have had better luck."

He started up and moodily drove away. I left him to his silence for a little way, then I said:

"You didn't think they'd take the stuff straight home?"

"Why not? They can't have known we were on to them. They might know now — it's surprising how the word gets round — but they wouldn't have known before. And I felt sure they'd have dropped it at Conway's place. That's why I picked this one when Atkinson offered me a choice. We all make mistakes."

"What made you guess it would be there?"

"Well, think about it, man. They thought they'd be in the clear. They didn't expect us to have any information. And the way they'd worked it out, Conway was going to be the unfortunate and honest security bloke who'd been jumped on by a gang of thugs. He wouldn't be suspected at all — or so they must have thought — so what better place to stash the stuff than Conway's house?"

"Why not Warburton's house? He's a jack. He didn't know he was suspected. I should have thought that was a better bet."

"Let's hope you're right, Peeper. And we'll find out in a minute. We're going back to Mortley Police Station to confer."

"When you say 'we', does that include me?"

"Why not? There'll be nobody there but bobbies, so you should be fairly safe. And you're about to be blown anyway."

★ ★ ★

In the exclusive view of Bert Boggis, nothing had been found at the other two houses either. I must say I didn't share his view, and Atkinson was at least half on my side. Warburton's house had yielded a police personal radio that wasn't signed out to him, but they thought that would be no more than a discipline offence, because he could plead forgetfulness, and they weren't very interested in chasing discipline matters. But at Harker's house they'd come up with what I would have considered a good haul. Harker was a bit of a hoarder, it seemed, and his bedroom was full of cameras, radios, clothing, wallets, jewellery, spirits, fags and God alone knows what else, all of it pinched from houses and shops in the town and most of it identifiable. But no silver, and that meant failure in Bert's eyes.

Atkinson was more concerned with the absence of bodies. Neither Warburton nor Harker had been found at home, and now that the thing was fully in the open it was odds-on they'd stay away.

"They must have had a tip-off, Bert," Atkinson said darkly.

"Looks like it. But how, for God's sake?"

"Aren't you forgetting the third man?" I suggested.

"What third man?" Atkinson said.

"Well, you found Conway tied up, didn't you? And he was in uniform. But back at the factory you said *three* masked men. I shouldn't have thought Conway would wear a mask if he was in his working gear."

Boggis and Atkinson exchanged looks.

"Thanks, Peeper. We'll bear that one in mind," Atkinson said. "And now, if you don't mind, you can get your thinking cap on, because you're going to make a long statement."

10

WHEN Atkinson talked about a long statement, he meant a long statement. The only saving grace about it was that I didn't have to do the writing. Atkinson did it himself, with Bert Boggis sitting at his elbow, both of them asking me questions as we went along. I don't know how long it took him to write it, but it must have taken him half an hour to read the bloody thing back to me before I signed it.

The larks were rubbing the sleep out of their eyes when Bert Boggis dropped me off. I knew it was the wrong time to go home — to Doreen's place, that is — so I got him to take me to the Albion Hotel.

He wouldn't go all the way, even at that hour. Boggis avoids the Albion like it was a smallpox ward. He still has unhappy memories of a time, years ago, when I'd known no better than to send him there to talk to Stella about some enquiry or other. I think I mentioned earlier that Stella hates cops — well the Boggis visit is a historic case in point. It seems she smiled at him till he said the magic words, 'I'm a police officer', and then she set about him with enough gusto to fetch plaster down off the walls. Bert departed with tail firmly between legs and with a promise ringing in his ears of permanent disablement if he ever showed his face — or any other part of him — there again.

I can't remember what the particular enquiry was, but I'll never forget the session I had with Boggis shortly after. I found him spitting blood and feathers, making out charge sheets for police assault, defamation and breach of the peace and laying on a dozen strong men to go and bring her in. It took me about an hour to talk him out of it, and he's hated the place ever since.

But I digress — and I really shouldn't do that.

Bert took me to within two streets of the Albion and I walked the rest. I let myself in through the back door, went upstairs and slid into the big bed alongside Stella. I'd had a long day and all I wanted was about twelve hours kip, so it suited me that Stella would be fast asleep and wouldn't want to make any new inroads on my stamina.

She wasn't — and she did. And refusing Stella is like telling the grass not to grow or the rain not to fall. By the time I got to sleep, I was one very weary man.

Maybe I'm boring you with these accounts of my somewhat non-conformist domestic activities, but I'm not doing it just to pass the time of day. I have to explain it now, because later on it becomes very relevant.

It was noon when I woke up, and after I'd fed and spruced myself up I set off to make repairs to the damaged bridgehead between me and Doreen.

Once again, this is just boring tittle-tattle and I don't intend to waste too much time describing it. Doreen wasn't playing is the short explanation. She was in all right, and we had a heated conversation through the letter box, but the bolts must have rusted up or something, because there was no way I could get that door open. I hadn't done enough penance yet, it seemed, and she didn't hold out any promises for a change of heart.

So I was stymied somewhat. I knew I could go back to the Albion later — hell, I could live at the Albion for ever if I really wanted to — but if I'd shown up there within half an hour of leaving there'd have been a raised eyebrow or two. Stella would have been pleased, but puzzled, and a puzzled Stella is an inquisitive Stella, a creature I couldn't face in my present state of mind.

Which I hope explains why I was reduced to killing time by walking about the streets. Which in turn leads me on to another part of this odd story.

I was strolling up Thorne Street, a sort of out-of-town shopping street with more houses than shops, where customers are thin on the ground. I was browsing in shop windows and otherwise minding my own business when I heard the motor bike approaching from behind and I didn't give it a second thought. You might have supposed that I'd be more interested, knowing what I knew, but motor bikes are common enough these days and you can't go round responding to every little noise you hear. Besides, my mind was full of Doreen and Stella and one or two other trivial matters. The result was, I only woke up when the damned thing was right on top of me, and by then it was almost too late.

I remember thinking he was going a bit fast, and I remember the sound of his engine seemed to be reaching me from the wrong side of the road — and I was absolutely right on both counts.

When I turned round, the bastard wasn't on the carriageway at all, he was on the pavement. And he was coming for me like a bullet. He was dressed in leathers and had one of those great robot bonce covers on, but the first is standard gear and the second required by law, so I couldn't read too much into that. But somehow I didn't think he'd missed his way. I thought he meant to be exactly where he was.

I did a stylish dance to get out of his path, but the way he followed me to and fro you'd have thought we were both in the same chorus line, and in a time sense I didn't have more than two beats to the bar. So I stopped dancing, flung myself off the pavement into the gutter and crawled like a baby towards the crown of the road. The bastard stayed right behind me.

What saved me, I think, was the height of the pavement edge which was a bit above par at that point. He was leaning right over in a curve and when his wheel went off the edge it twisted and threw him into a wobble. By the time he'd righted himself he was out of line and although he was going for my head or my guts he only managed to bounce over my foot. It gave me a hell of a bang and some part of the bike hooked in my trouser leg and ripped it straight up to the knee, but when I climbed up and tried my weight on it the foot seemed to be O.K. Sore as hell, but O.K.

Before then the bike had sheered off and was hurtling away up the street, but I had time for a quick glimpse of the number, and having had cause to check it twice before I had no doubts whatever this time.

Shaun Harker. The bastard.

Thinking back on the incident I know what I should have done. I should have rushed into the nearest shop, grabbed a phone, dialled three nines and slipped the leash on every hound Boggis had in his pack. But I wasn't thinking straight at the time. I was all shook up, my foot was starting to hurt like mad and my pants leg was flapping in the breeze. Moreover, I was superlatively and comprehensively angry. The little shit had tried to kill me, I was certain of that, and what I wanted more than anything else in the world was a pair of pincers with Harker's balls in the jaws.

So I ran after him, waving my fists in the air and shocking the populace with the variety of my vocabulary. I was so intent on racing him to the top of the street that I forgot the pain in my foot. We all do foolish things sometimes — me more than most. If I say he managed to pull ahead you'll appreciate what I mean. But rage had started me off and rage kept me going, even though I hadn't a fly's chance in a Flit factory of catching him.

Fifty yards up the street I came on a bread van with its engine running — and it was pointing in the right direction.

Now I've nicked a car or two in my time, I must admit, but I've never committed a theft as blatant as that one, either before or since. The bread salesman was right there, loading trays in the back, when I shoved his van in gear and raced away in a Le Mans start. I heard the doors swinging and crashing behind me and I suppose I scattered a bread roll or two, but I didn't care a damn. I just gripped the wheel and trod hard on the gas.

There was nobody in my way as luck would have it. There were no vehicles claiming their right of way at the next intersection, or the next, or the next. I went through at least two sets of traffic lights on red, surprised an old lady on a zebra crossing and caused a passing cyclist (me passing him, that is) to fall off his machine. It wasn't me driving at all — it was a raving screaming maniac of a bloke who used to be me. I built that van up to a speed it had probably never attained before in all its puff and if it had exploded that wouldn't have bothered me, because I didn't give a damn for anything or anybody else.

I just wanted Harker, preferably right under my front wheels.

Harker had the legs of me, of course, but he wasn't prepared to drive as recklessly as I was, which restored the balance a bit. I caught a glimpse of him very early on and managed to hold him in sight for maybe a mile. Whether he ever realized I was after him or not I simply don't know, but he certainly shook me off. After that glorious mile, during which I had high hopes of coming to very painful grips with him, he went out of my sight and was lost for ever.

I slowed down after a while, but kept on driving in the same direction till I was way out in the country. I'd cooled down a bit by then and was starting to think more clearly. I didn't have a ghost of a chance of finding him again. He might have gone just about anywhere. I might as well stop wasting my time. So I turned the van round and drove back towards town at a much more sedate pace. I wasn't even searching any more, and it was only by sheer chance that I noticed wheel tracks turning off the main road into a side lane.

I stopped and got out to check. They were motor bike tyre marks all right. The machine had passed through a puddle just short of the turning and the marks were still showing wet. I could see the single line of tread pattern in the road and the long shallow loop of double track where he'd laid her over to take the corner. Somebody had ridden a motor bike over this spot very recently, and he'd been going in, not coming out, otherwise the wet marks would have been on the opposite side of the puddle.

But was it Harker?

It didn't have to be him. In fact, if I'd been running a book on it I'd have had to give long odds. In this district, and maybe every other district for all I know you can count motor bikes in batches of a hundred and it'll take you quite a while to count them all. But there had to be an outside chance, and I was in the market for a chance. So I climbed back into the bread van, backed up a yard or two and nosed into the lane. Two hundred yards in, it crossed the canal. I went over the humpbacked bridge and drove on for perhaps another mile. The lane seemed to lead nowhere except to a couple of isolated farms and anyway I'd had my fill of it by then, so I turned in a gateway and set off for home.

Coming back up the lane I saw a police car flash past on the main road, heading out of town and going like the clappers. Not being stupid, I allowed he might be looking for me. Chances were that every police car on the road was looking for me, or at least for the bread van thief, which amounted to the same thing. So I turned back the way he'd come, and at the first lay-by I came to I ditched the van and set off on foot. It would have been a long walk back, but I had no intention of walking all the way. At the first telephone kiosk

I rang Boggis and told him it would be in his best interests to come and pick me up.

He didn't sound any notes of sympathy about my sore foot or my damaged trousers. The best he could offer was a needle and thread and an elastoplast. I told him to stitch his great silly mouth up with the first and bung the second over to keep the first in place.

Give Boggis his due though, he never batted an eyelid when I talked about chasing Harker in a van. He asked a lot of questions about the incident in Thorne Street and other connected matters — kept on at me for ages about all that — but he never asked me anything about the van.

I think he knew — and didn't want to know — if you see what I mean.

11

I SPENT the next few hours closeted with Boggis, We did an awful lot of talking — and most of it came from him.

I must stop saying unkind things about Bert. He's not all bad. Usually, when he's deeply into a job of some importance, he becomes preoccupied with it and refuses to be led off on a diverging path. But this time, after he'd listened to my story, I got the feeling he was giving some priority to my little problem. He seemed very put out by the thought that Shaun Harker had had a go at me, and he came nearer to fussing over me than I've ever known him come before.

"That was nothing less than attempted murder," he snarled.

I must confess, I hadn't looked at it quite like that, but thinking back I could only agree with him. I'd come to no lasting harm, but if Harker had had a bit more luck — or I'd had a bit less — I might have finished up with something more than a sore foot.

"He was doing his best, Bert," I said.

"So he was. And that raises a problem for me, Peeper."

"How so? I thought it only raised a problem for me."

"He committed a crime, and a very serious one. The question is, do I put it on paper, or do I keep it up my sleeve?"

"I'm not with you, Bert. Does it make any difference?"

"Let me put it this way. There's a big shindig going on down at Mortley. They've set up a murder room and the whole town is full of coppers knocking on doors. I'm helping out — and we've got detectives scouring this town too — but it isn't my job, because it's off my patch. Now, all of a sudden, I've got my own job — a murderous attack on you — and we know very well that it's linked up with theirs. So there's no question about it, Peeper. What I ought to do is get straight through to the Detective Chief Superintendent at Mortley and tell him all about this new development."

"That sounds reasonable. Why don't you do it?"

"I'm thinking about it. But if I do it, it brings you out into the open, and I'm not sure that would be a wise thing to do. It's not just a matter of telling them, you see. It also involves putting crime forms in, sending messages and circulating our friend Harker as wanted for attempted murder. The minute I do that, the circus is going to descend on me. They'll grab you and put you through the mill, they'll swamp Thorne Street with bobbies, and before you know where you are they'll be hearing stories about vans and that sort of thing. That might make things unpleasant for you, and it's a mess I'd rather avoid."

"What's the alternative?"

"That's easy. You don't tell me about it."

"That's bloody ridiculous. I've already told you."

"I know that, but they don't. Now don't misunderstand me, Peeper. I'm not suggesting we sit on this for ever. It's bound to come out in the wash, and when it does I'll see that bloody man Harker do time for it. But it would suit my purposes, and yours, and the police at Mortley in the long run, if you delayed making an official complaint. That way, I won't have to take any official action till I'm good and ready. When the time comes, you can make your complaint, and that will be the first I've heard about it."

"It suits me, Bert. You can play it how you like."

"Good. That's settled then. But when the time comes, Peeper, you'll have to back me up. If you ever squeal that you told me earlier, I'll have to deny it, because what I'm doing amounts to neglect of duty, and they can sack policemen for that, even sergeants."

"I never said a word, Bert. I didn't think it worth mentioning."

"It's agreed then. And now that we've agreed I know nothing about it we can get down to discussing it. Harker takes a big risk by attacking you in the street, but he must think the risk worth taking. You know why that is, I suppose?"

"To begin with, it means he doesn't like me."

"It means a lot more than that, Peeper. It means he fears you. He has you taped as the danger man. He was trying to eliminate you, that's my guess, and it follows that he must think he'll be safer with you out of the way."

"That sounds like a good reason, Bert. But at the same time it sounds bloody impossible. How could he have found out?"

"Well, let's work on it. I think the first thing to remember is that

Warburton and Harker are in this thing together. Even though most of your dealings were with Warburton, not Harker."

"They were all with Warburton really. The only time I saw Harker was right at the beginning, in Vince Skinner's place. That's as far as he knows, anyway. And even then he only stood by while Warburton talked to me."

"I know that. But the point I'm making is that we mustn't be misled by that. It's very easy to assume that Harker knows only the bits he was involved in, but we should put that out of our minds. We have to accept that Harker knows as much as Warburton, because Warburton will certainly have told him. On that basis, Harker knows you work with me. He knows you were instrumental in recovering that first load of silver. He knows you set up a job with Warburton that involved Conway. He knows everything that went on when you had your meetings with Warburton in his car. And he also knows that, having gone through the charade of arresting Conway, Warburton subsequently told you a pack of lies about the raid being a failure."

"I accept all of that, Bert, but it still doesn't clear my mind. I want to argue the opposite. Harker can't possibly know *more* than Warburton knows, and neither of them knows I stood behind that fence and watched them pick up Conway. They don't know I ever saw them with a gun either. Without knowing those things, how can they possibly have enough to start blaming me?"

"I think they worked it out. Probably from what happened last night. Put yourself in their position for a minute. They believe they have a foolproof plan. They go down to the Bragg-Norton place and with Conway's help they pull off a big job. Up to then, everything seems to have gone well. Nobody has any idea that they're behind it — not even you — because although Warburton has been using you, he's still playing the policeman, still chasing drugs and blue films, and he hasn't as much as hinted to you about a raid on the Bragg-Norton factory.

"So, when Warburton and Harker depart with the silver, leaving Conway trussed up in his office, they're entitled to suppose they've got clean away with it. Conway thinks the same. And then look what happens. They've barely cleared the place when the police arrive, mob-handed, and burst in to the rescue. I imagine that shook Conway, because as boss man of night security he knew damned well nobody had sent for the police. They'd just turned up — like magic — to save him, when he'd been expecting to lie bound and gagged till the morning shift arrived.

"Well, he'd write that off as pure chance, or an illustration of police efficiency, and he'd quietly thank his stars that his buddies were well off the premises. He'd wait for the bobbies to untie him, cluck sympathy at him and put his name up for an Industrial Grand Star of Valour, or some such. After which he'd wander round the place saying things like, *Oh dear they've shot my two best men*, and, *Oh dear they've pinched all the silver*.

"They untie him anyway, he was quite right about that, but imagine his surprise when Detective Inspector Atkinson bends over him as soon as the gag's off, without any preliminaries, and says, *Denzil Conway, I arrest you for murder and theft*, or something of that order. He must have had a duck-fit. And it doesn't stop there, because shortly afterwards we take him to his house, strip the place clean and take away all his funny powders and his pretty pictures of schoolgirls being raped.

"Make no mistake, Peeper. After that, Conway has got the message. He may not know how it came about, but he knows fine well that somebody has put the squeak in.

"Meanwhile, back at the ranches — that's Warburton's place and Harker's place — much the same sort of thing is happening. It starts to rain policemen, rude policemen with big feet and heavy hands. They go through those houses like a dose of salts and they leave the occupiers in no doubt that their loving sons — Harker and Warburton — are very much wanted men. Now all three of them have got the message, first Conway, then the other two. We haven't worked it out yet, Peeper, but in some way, Warburton and Harker seem to have known in advance, because they'd cleared off before we got there."

"Warburton used that pocket radio," I suggested. That struck me as a good idea, but Boggis shook his head.

"No he didn't."

"How do you know that?"

"Because we've checked it out. Hell's teeth, Peeper, do give us a bit of credit. The minute that radio was found in Warburton's house its possibilities were

230

ripped apart, analysed and put back together again. We know he didn't use the radio, because no messages about the Bragg-Norton job were ever passed over the air. Mr. Atkinson was careful about that. He didn't have to use radio, so he left it alone. It's a common practice among thinking policemen. Its purpose is to thwart certain Press reporters who listen in. And by coincidence, it thwarted Warburton."

"There could have been a second message passed out, just for Warburton."

"Be careful what you're saying, Peeper. You're suggesting that some other police officer was involved."

"I didn't say that."

"You implied it though, because the radio, like most forms of communication, requires somebody at both ends. And it calls for a radio at both ends too, which almost certainly means some other policeman."

"Well, it's possible, isn't it?"

"It's very possible, and that bothers

me. You can rest assured we're making enquiries in that direction. But not in relation to radio calls. We know he didn't use that radio."

Boggis was making fun of me. His face hadn't cracked at all, but I could see that characteristic twitch of lip and cheek.

"Go on. I'll buy it."

"The thing was flat as a pancake. Duff batteries."

"He could have switched the batteries."

"Oh do give over. He couldn't, as a matter of fact. The thing had batteries in but they were corroded to all hell. They had to be prised out. No, you can write the radio off as a red herring. We tested it all ways. It was inoperative.

"But we're straying from the subject. The point is, all three of them knew they'd been rumbled. It didn't matter in Conway's case, because he was safely locked away, but the other two were still loose. And as soon as Warburton and Harker put their heads together they figured it out, no trouble. It had to be you, Peeper. It couldn't have been anybody else."

"So Harker sets out to get rid of me?"

"They both do, legally speaking. Harker was the instrument, but both were guilty — assuming it could be proved. Not Conway though. He's in the clear. He couldn't have conspired with them on that one. Though he did with the factory job, of course. But it's Warburton and Harker who are the arch villains. Denzil Conway was trapped into the scheme."

"What makes you say he was trapped?"

"You're pulling my leg aren't you? That bit's as clear as crystal. I should have thought you'd have worked it out."

"Well I haven't — so tell me."

"It's an oft told story, Peeper. We can safely say that this whole scheme started that day when we used Warburton to buy back that first load of stolen silver. Up to then he was just a working detective. Not the most reliable man, I gather, but there's no reason to believe he was involved in any criminal escapades. But he saw that silver and liked the look of it, and then at a later stage he found out there was a lot more where that came from."

"How did he find that out?"

"He saw it, when the first lot was being handed back to the company. Detective Inspector Atkinson returned the stuff, but Warburton went with him. The bloke they handed it back to — and who signed the official receipt, was Denzil Conway. Conway, by the way, is second-in-command of the security staff there. He and the Chief Security Officer work alternate shifts, and when the first load was handed back, Conway happened to be on duty. That was fate, I suppose. The Devil working towards his evil ends. At that stage, Conway wasn't involved in any fiddle — and he was dealing with the police, remember, who are supposed to be trustworthy — so he didn't think twice about showing Mr. Atkinson and Warburton through to the main metal compound, to put back the load they'd just returned. Warburton picked up two little useful snippets there. He noted that Conway had unrestricted access to the place — and he also saw the rest of the silver. Mr. Atkinson tells me the stuff's stacked up in pyramids, like butter in a supermarket."

"And that sparked off Warburton's plan?"

"It gave him the germ of the idea, anyway. I guess he started suffering from greed — as most policemen do from time to time. The difference is that Warburton didn't resist it. He succumbed to temptation."

"And slipped a proposition in to Conway?"

"Hell, no. That's the very point. Warburton did nothing at first, but he must have gone around afterwards with visions of that silver mountain haunting him night and day. And somewhere along the line, he teamed up with Harker."

"Shaun Harker's a funny chum for a policeman."

"Yes, but a chum of long standing, I gather. They've known each other since they played together as kids. And later on, when they both got the motor bike craze, they started to see a lot of each other."

"Even though Warburton knew Harker was a thief?"

"Yes. And even though Harker knew Warburton was a policeman. Between you and me, Peeper, I think that alone stamps Warburton for what he is — an unprincipled bloody rogue. I've known a lot of coppers who've had boyhood associations with people who grew up to be crooks. I'm in that category myself, as a matter of fact, and I'm not talking about present company. But any copper worth his salt would keep his bent acquaintances at arm's length. He'd remember his position and he'd steer clear. But not friend Warburton. He cultivated Harker, in spite of them being on the opposite sides of the fence."

"And as it turns out, they were both on the same side."

"That's right. Warburton's a renegade, a classic case. But let me get back to the story. Warburton nursed his hopes about the silver and kept them warm. Likely as not, he shared them with Harker, but whether he did that at an early stage or only when the opportunity came his way we'll probably never know. The point is, Warburton kept his eyes open, and before long he got the black on Conway."

"And I was the one who got it for him."

"No, I don't think that's the case. You certainly clinched it for him, but he already had the information before he came to you. I suspect he found out in the course of his job. Somebody went to Warburton — some disgruntled but public-spirited citizen I suppose — and tipped him the wink that there was something funny going on at that house. It must have been manna from Heaven for Warburton, especially when he found it was Conway's house and remembered who Conway was. It gave him the very chance he'd been waiting for."

"I can see that, Bert. But what do you suppose gave him the idea of coming to me for help?"

"A combination of things, I'd say. Almost certainly he'd make his own enquiries first. He probably got the whisper that it was a drugs and blue films case but couldn't confirm it. I'm quite sure if he could have collected the evidence himself he would never have involved anybody else."

"Except Harker, of course."

"Maybe not even Harker — who knows? But he needed to be absolutely certain of all the background to Conway's activities before he could risk dropping in on Conway. His motives are important at this stage. Working as a policeman, no doubt he'd have taken a chance, as we all have to do sometimes, but Warburton wasn't working as a policeman — he was working for his own ends. From experience, he knew very well that police raids frequently abort, and he couldn't risk an abortion with this one, because too many of his personal ambitions hung in the balance.

"So he came to you. And thinking about it, I'm very pleased he did. Because if he hadn't, we wouldn't have been forewarned. We'd have heard nothing at all about the job till morning. Conway would have made his story stick, and between them they might have pulled off the perfect crime.

"But it's fairly evident that he couldn't come up with the clincher by working on his own. He was a local jack, remember, and he couldn't go undercover himself, because his face was well known and too many people might have recognized him. So he cast around for somebody to do his dirty work for him, and that's when he came to you."

"But why me, Bert? It doesn't make sense. Apart from that silver job he'd had no previous dealings with me. I'd never even spoken to Warburton before. And I should have thought Harker could have dug the facts out for him just as well as me. And cheaper, because he was already part of the fiddle."

"We don't know he was. He might not even have mentioned it to Harker at that stage. Or maybe Harker was known, locally, to be knocking round with a detective. The point is, he didn't use Harker — he used you."

"I still don't understand why."

"I'm guessing now, but I think it was because of the sort of work involved. Don't get all swell-headed about it, but I think he wanted an experienced man. Harker wasn't experienced enough. Of course, Warburton might have used one of his own informants — assuming he has any — but they'd be Mortley people and he'd prefer to use somebody from outside Mortley. When he started thinking that way, he must have remembered you. At the time of the first silver job, he'd seen you sitting in my car. He guessed you were working with me, and that meant you were reliable, so he came to sound you out."

"Wasn't he playing with fire, Bert? I might have come straight to you and blown his little scheme wide open."

"No. He had good reason to believe you wouldn't do that. Two good reasons, in fact. He wasn't going to talk to you about silver — only about drugs and blue films, and the chances of you linking that stuff with a silver raid were negligible. We know, now, that he never did tell you anything more. And he even scotched the drugs and blue films job by telling you it had come to nothing. He wasn't to know that you'd see through him in an unexpected way."

"That's one reason. What's the other?"

Boggis paused and gave me a sideways look. I couldn't tell whether he was serious or joking.

"You were ratting on me, you treacherous little sod. You were doing a crafty deal on the side, for money. Warburton knew damned well — or thought he did — that once he'd greased your palm there was no way you'd ever say anything to me."

"He was nearly right, too," I admitted. "If I hadn't seen the danger signs I never would have told you."

"You think I don't know that? You'd have milked him for everything he had — as you've done with me all these years — but that's past and more or less forgotten. The point is, you helped to foster his visions of great wealth. You did a great job on Conway, Peeper, I'll give you that. Armed with the information you gave him, Warburton could have laid on a raid through proper channels. It would have been a good lift for a young detective, a feather in his cap, but it wasn't half as good as a load of silver, and Warburton wanted that silver."

"So he let Conway off the hook?"

"That's it exactly. Instead of an official raid, he laid on an unofficial one, using Harker. That was a piece of boldness if you like. It was bloody foolhardy — but it worked. You'd have thought even Conway would smell a rat when only two men turned up to do a job like that — and for him to believe two, he had to accept, at least in the initial stages, that Shaun Harker was a bobby. He doesn't look much like a bobby to me."

"So it could easily have gone wrong, right at the outset."

"It could have, but it didn't. They caught Conway bang to rights with his narcotics and his naughty nuns, and Conway must have believed he was nicked official. When they took him off in the car, he must have believed he was on his way to the police station — as he would have been in any straight arrest — but they never went anywhere near the police station. You can see how it must have happened. Somewhere along the route, Warburton parked up and he and Harker started working on Conway. They painted his crimes as black as they could, threatened him with every punishment in the penal system and kept loading the pressure on till they scared the shit right out of him and had him looking forward to a public hanging.

"That was when Warburton played his ace card, I suppose. He offered Conway a deal, and he must have made it sound good, because Conway snatched at the chance."

"But Conway might have refused to play. What would they have done if he'd told them to get lost?"

"That would have changed the picture, sure. I don't know how they'd have tackled that. I don't think even Warburton would have had the nerve to take Conway in and charge him, not after they'd given him an outline of the scheme. And particularly not when the only supporting witness was a rotten little thief like Harker. But we needn't blow our minds working that one out, because the problem didn't arise. Conway must have liked the scheme. He chucked in his lot with them."

"And he was a security officer. It doesn't say much for his character."

"Character, Peeper? Don't make me smile. Denzil Conway never had a character worth a row of pins. He was already corrupt before Warburton latched on to him. You went to his place, so you know damned well what he did with his spare time. And don't forget, it was Conway who supplied the gun — or at any rate we have to assume that, from what you saw."

"When you think of it that way . . ."

"That's the only way you can think

of it. Conway was the ideal accomplice for Warburton and Harker. He had no morals worth a light. He was deep into commerce of the wrong kind. He was just as greedy as the others, and best of all he had the run of the Bragg-Norton factory."

"I'm surprised he didn't nick the silver himself."

"It wouldn't have been practical. Just as Warburton needed Conway, Conway needed Warburton, or somebody like him. Working at the place, Conway could only help himself if at the same time he appeared to be completely innocent, and that was what the scheme was designed to bring about.

"I don't mind admitting, the plan was good. Old and well used, but still good. This business of tying the watchman up, or the lorry driver, or the shop manager, is pretty standard stuff. We're always suspicious, but we can't always be sure. It's been done thousands of times, and in a lot of cases I'm sure it's genuine — the watchman or whatever really is innocent — but not always, because we know of hundreds of cases where it's come unstuck, and I suspect there are hundreds more cases that are bogus, but we never find out.

"You see, Peeper. If the watchman sticks to his story it can be a damned difficult story to break. We'd have had our work cut out in the present case. Conway's a tough little sod. If we hadn't known the truth in advance, there's no telling how we'd have cracked it. We might have had to believe his story, especially since two of his mates had been shot."

"Is he admitting it now?"

"He wasn't, last time I checked, and maybe he never will. But we'll stitch him up in the end."

"Using me?"

"Using you, if we must."

"So you're home and dry then. The job's over."

"Over? Whatever are you babbling about, Peeper? How the hell can it be over when we still haven't got

Warburton, haven't got Harker and haven't got the silver? No. There's a lot to be done yet. And you can gird your loins, because we're just about to start."

12

"STICK with me, Peeper," Boggis said, "and maybe you'll learn something. This is very unorthodox. For a while, I'll be playing both sides against the middle, but it's in a good cause and I've got the interests of the job at heart. You're not supposed to be here, so you mustn't make a sound, but when I pick this phone up, shove your head alongside. You'll get the gist."

Boggis dialled a number and asked to be connected with the police at Mortley. When the switchboard answered, he asked for Detective Inspector Atkinson. Atkinson turned out to be in Murder Control and the call was put through. He came on the line, said *hello*, and named himself.

"Sergeant Boggis here, sir. I'm on the cadge for a progress report."

"I wish I could give you one, Bert, but there's not a lot of progress so far. There's good news about our second security guard, the one who was shot in the arm. He'd lost a lot of blood, but they tell me it's not that serious and he's on the mend."

"Very gratifying. I'm glad he's no worse. But I was being practical. I've nothing fresh at this end. How about you?"

"Still struggling. Warburton and Harker have gone to ground."

"No reports of sightings?"

"Not so far, and I've got patrols on every major road. They haven't tried to go back home either, or to Conway's place. I've got a watch on all three. But they'll fall eventually, Bert. And when they do, we'll have enough to give them a run."

"What's the state of the poll with Conway?"

"We've charged him with the lot. He was in Court an hour ago and we got him remanded to cells. He's got a solicitor, of course. A funny sort of bloke from out of town. He won't leave his client alone. Keeps giving him the stock advice, to keep his mouth shut."

"He's that sort, is he? We're in the wrong trade, you and I. It must be a damned sight easier to put a clamp on a bloke's tongue than to try to worm things out of him."

Atkinson chuckled.

"I don't know, Bert. I wouldn't have this chap's job for a pension. He can't stop us asking questions and we keep grinding away at Conway. And although he keeps telling Conway not to answer the questions, he's getting nowhere. Conway can't take advice."

"You don't mean he's making admissions?"

"Better than that, in my view. He keeps telling lies, Bert. He wants to protest his innocence from the housetops, so he keeps telling us all about how it didn't happen. And the man's a fool to himself. He keeps making mistakes, then correcting them. The trouble for him, though he doesn't realize it, is that he's trying to invent things as he goes along and he doesn't do it well. I have high hopes that he'll really shop himself in the end."

"He can't deny the films and things."

"No. He'll nod his head to those charges when the time comes. Even his solicitor has advised him to make a clean breast of the lesser offences. But it's the big one we're after, so it's a case of waiting till he oversteps himself properly."

"You'll have asked him about the gun?"

"Oh yes. He denies all knowledge of it. The ruffians who attacked him brought it with them. He doesn't know about guns. He hasn't the slightest idea what type it was, or what it looked like. On the credit side, we've recovered two slugs and they've gone off to the Lab., for a ballistics check, but it'll be a day or two before we get a report back. You haven't found it, I suppose?"

"I've found nothing at this end, but I'm still trying. Is there anything special lined up for me to do?"

"No. Except keep trying, and keep in touch."

"That's fine then. I'll let you know if I hear anything."

★ ★ ★

"You'll kindly forgive me for telling those lies, Peeper," he said as he hung the phone up. "If you think I like misleading Len Atkinson you can think again. He'll have no cause to grumble by the time I've finished. And now — we might have shut the shop on this little sideline of yours, but we're still going to investigate it. How sure are you that it was Harker who ran you down?"

"I can't be sure, can I. With that great lump of plastic on his head, he could have been anybody. But it was his bike all right. I won't forget that number in a hurry."

"That's what I was really asking. Are you sure about the number?"

"Absolutely. I know it off by heart."

"Let's hear it then — just as a check."

I told him the number and he wrote it down. Then he turned to a scrap pad on his desk and made a comparison.

"It's Harker's all right. That's the number you asked me to check for you a few days ago, and here's the computer read-out. I wish you'd levelled with me then, Peeper. It might have saved both of us a lot of trouble."

"I don't see how. It was just a curiosity then. Nothing to write home about. We couldn't have foreseen how things would develop."

"Maybe you're right. Anyway, it's water under the bridge. Now these tracks you mentioned. Do you think they were made by Harker?"

"Your guess is as good as mine. If you're asking for my guess — no, I don't think so."

"Why not?"

"Well, what I really mean is, there's nothing to point that way. You can't stand on any street-end without seeing a motor bike pass by and any one of them might have made those marks."

"But whoever he was, Peeper, he was in the right area, at the right time and going in the right direction. That narrows the field down a bit. And since we're looking for motor bikes we ought to check it out. It's the only lead we've got."

"You'd be looking for one apple in a barrel."

"I agree completely. But if you want your apple you've got to search for it. That's police work. The way you search a barrel of apples for one particular apple is not to delve in and scrabble through. You pick up a single apple and examine it. If it doesn't fit the one you're looking for you chuck it on the reject pile and tick it off the list. That way, eventually, you come to the right apple. And we can tell this one if we see it, because it has a number stamped on it, and we know that number."

"We're looking for two motor bikes."

"But it's odds on that they're both together, so if we find one we find both. Now stop fighting me, Peeper, you're overruled. We're going out to hunt that apple."

Boggis went to a cupboard, took out an ordnance survey map and returned to spread it out on his desk.

"Now this is the area. Can you point out that lane?"

I had to choose between several possibilities, but by a process of elimination I was able to stab my finger at one.

"That's it, Bert. I'm nearly sure. I can't be absolutely sure without going there to see, but I think I'm right."

"Let's take it that you are." He bent to the map and began to trace the lane with his finger. "It crosses the canal in a straight line. The main track goes right along here to a farm, Grant's Lee Farm, and it seems to end in the farmyard. But back here a piece there's a right-hand fork. That goes to, let me see, Humble Man Farm. But it doesn't stop there. It goes a bit further, as far as Keeper's Cottage, and then it stops. There's a line leading on from there, but it's only a footpath. Well, Peeper, there aren't many places to check, so it shouldn't take long. It's a dead end. There should have been a sign at the junction saying so — a 'No Through Road' sign. Can you remember seeing one?"

"Not that I noticed."

"It doesn't matter. Grab your coat, mate. We're on our way."

★ ★ ★

"Don't tell me you're just going to crash in there and knock on doors," I objected as we were bowling along in Bert's old banger. "Because if you are, I think you're bloody mad."

"Why so? This is a civilized country. They won't eat us."

"They might shoot us. Have you forgotten the gun?"

There was a short, uneasy silence and I thought I had him.

"Look on the bright side, Peeper," he said eventually. "If Warburton and Harker are not there, there's no harm done."

"And if they are?"

"Well, that's what we're after, isn't it? If they're there, and they show themselves, we shan't have to bother checking any other apples."

I'd chosen the right lane, and there was a traffic sign at its entrance, just as Boggis had predicted. He steamed down the lane at his usual breakneck speed and I was quite surprised when he braked hard just before the canal bridge and pulled onto the grass.

"You seen something?"

"Not yet. But I'm going to have a look."

He climbed out of the car and I followed him. He stood on the bridge for a short while and gazed along the towing path in both directions. Then he said:

"I think I've got a case, Peeper. Damn it, I'm sure I have."

"What sort of case?"

"Driving a motor vehicle on the towing-path. That's a breach of the National Waterways byelaws. You can be fined for it."

"Big deal. I hope you get a medal for being bright."

"Seriously, old mate. It does look interesting. Step this way and we'll have a closer look. Unless I'm very much mistaken, that motor vehicle only had two wheels. There's hardly room for a car, and anyway, who'd drive a car along a bloody canal?"

The entrance to the canal towing-path was right there beside the bridge, a ramp sloping down from the tarmac strip of the lane. The ramp itself was hard and dry, gravelly and grass-grown, but at the bottom where it opened onto the towing path there was a band of spongy earth, and the marks were plain to see at that point.

"Looks like it was a car, Bert."

"Correction. It was more than one motor bike — or maybe the same motor bike more than once. Look at the tracks, man. They haven't had tyres as narrow as that on cars since the Baby Austin. It's these two tracks that are fooling you. They're the right width apart, but they're not parallel. Just follow the lines they take. If they continued on at that rake, they'd come to a point inside thirty yards. And now look between those two. There's more tracks. Quite a lot more. There's been a fair few motor bikes over this spot — a regular full-scale scramble."

"Maybe that's what it was — a scramble?"

"And maybe it was those bastards Warburton and Harker."

"You want to take it slower, Bert. You're getting excited. There's a fair chance that the bike that left the tracks at the lane-end turned down here. But that doesn't mean it was the one we're after. All sorts of odd people might want to break those daft byelaws. Fishermen, hunters, farmers, anybody."

"They're obviously heading north," Boggis said, ignoring me. "There aren't any marks turning back under the bridge, and there would have been if anybody had gone that way. It's damp enough. So the thing to do, Peeper, is have another look at that map. Come on. I've got it in the car."

There was nothing of significance on the north side of the bridge — not for a fair distance anyway. The canal kept going for ever, and I've no doubt it passed all sorts of towns and villages on the way, but looking at the first mile or two there was only fields, hedges, woods and a few more canal bridges. I don't know what Boggis hoped to find, but he didn't find it.

"Come on, Peeper," he said, folding the map. "There's only one way to know for certain, and that's to ask the people who live in these parts. We'll try Humble Man Farm for a kick off."

★ ★ ★

I didn't enjoy that short drive up to the farm. The way I saw it, there was a one-in-three shot that Warburton and his mate would be there — and if they were, they'd recognize Boggis and me straight off, knowing both of us. It was always possible that they'd elect to lie low and wait for us to leave, but they might not. They might come out with guns blazing, and I might not be quick enough to hide behind Boggis. Nothing happened. The old Ford Consul rolled into a loose-cobbled yard, scattering ducks and chickens, and we climbed out in an atmosphere of peace.

The farmer's name was Billy Peacock and he seemed a friendly type. His look stayed friendly, even after Boggis had thrown his standard line of introduction, so I guessed he must like coppers.

"You got any motor bikes on the farm?" Boggis said chattily.

"Not runners. I've got a clapped-out old B.S.A. behind the barn, and I've a motor bike engine driving my swill pump."

"We're looking for the modern sort. Japanese. You know, the big flashy models that look like space ships."

"You've come to the wrong shop, then."

"Anybody ride one in these parts? Visitors? Reps?"

"Not that I've seen. You could try Harry Pickavance down at Keeper's Cottage. He had one a while back. But he hasn't got it now, I can tell you. Couldn't master it, he said. Sold it."

"There's another farm across yonder . . . I forget the name."

"Grant's Lee. Old Jacob Hilton's place. You can forget Old Jacob. He just has a van — and that's dropping to bits."

"It's not so much the farmers I'm thinking about," Boggis said. "I'm more interested in casuals; people who don't live here but maybe stay for a few days. You've got nobody like that?"

"Not at present. The wife did bed-and-breakfast for a while, but it didn't bring much custom, so she packed it in."

"Maybe it's one of the other places then. This Grant's Lee Farm — or Keeper's Cottage. I suppose I'd better check."

"Look, Sergeant," Peacock said. "It's none of my business, but if you're talking about motor bikes being driven around, you'd waste your time at those other places. Old Jacob's the sort who blasts off at callers with his twelve-bore. He's been up in court once for it. And Harry Pickavance can barely look after himself, let alone visitors."

"I'd better go and ask though, just to be sure."

"Suit yourself. But I was going to

say this. There's no motor bike ever goes this way to Keeper's Cottage, or I'd have seen it. They're noisy bloody things, so I couldn't miss. The lane runs straight past my door. And I'd nearly swear there's none ever goes to Jacob's place either. The road to his place is just across that paddock. You can see for yourself."

"They might have passed when you were out."

"Aye, that's possible. I go out once a week, for about an hour, so they could creep past then. But they couldn't roar past, that's for sure, or the wife would hear, and she'd tell me."

"I was wondering about the canal towing-path," Boggis said.

"Now then, you might have more chance there. I can't see anything unless I'm up that end, but there's a fair bit of traffic gets along there — that I do know."

"What sort of traffic?"

"Every sort. Cycles mostly. But I have seen the odd motor bike and a few cars. I once saw an army truck, one of those big green canvas jobs, but that bugger got stuck and had to be dragged out backwards."

"You surprise me, Mr. Peacock. It'll take cars then?"

"Oh aye. You should see it on a summer evening. Courting couples. You get two or three parked there sometimes." He chuckled as he reminisced. "And then if the lot in the front car finish first, they can't get out. I've listened to a shouting match or two yonder. Sometimes they have to drive straight through and come off at the next bridge."

"Courting couples. Well, I suppose that makes sense. Because we checked the map just now, and there doesn't seem to be anything up that way that they might want to get to."

"There's the fishing, and the shooting. And then there's always the quarry. You get all sorts in there. Boy Scouts, ramblers, blackberry pickers. There's a caravan there too, stuck in a field just past the quarry. I believe one of your blokes has that."

"One of our blokes? You mean a policeman?"

"Aye, a bobby. A young chap. You mean you didn't know?"

"That's right, Mr. Peacock. I didn't know."

"You do surprise me. Wait on though. Did you say you were local? Well this one isn't. He's stationed over at Mortley, I do believe, so chances are you won't have come across him."

"I'm not sure. If I heard the name, maybe I'd know him."

"His name's . . . hell, I should know it, but I can't think on. I should think the wife would know. Want me to ask her?"

"If you wouldn't mind. It's always useful to have names."

Boggis gave me some very odd looks while we were waiting for Peacock, but he didn't say anything and neither did I. The farmer came back with a triumphant expression on his face.

"Dinsdale," he said. "That's his name. And dammit, I should have remembered. I was in the army with a chap called Dinsdale. Not the same though. Different chap altogether."

"I've heard of a Dinsdale, I think. What's his first name?"

"Now that I can't tell you. And the wife doesn't know either."

"It doesn't matter, Mr. Peacock. Maybe I don't know him after all. You've been a big help with the motor bikes though, and I don't think we need to bother any further."

We were back in the Consul and moving off, when Peacock chased after us, shouting. Boggis stopped and wound the window down.

"I might have put you wrong there," Peacock said. "There is this caravan like I told you, but Dinsdale wouldn't get to it along the towing-path."

"There's no through road, is that what you mean?"

"There's a through road all right, but he wouldn't go that way. Why

268

squeeze along a bloody towing-path when there's a good wide track down to it? It runs off the main road, about a mile up."

★ ★ ★

Boggis clattered back up the lane with his foot hard down. The Consul bounced in the air as we crossed the canal bridge, but he didn't slow down. At the main road he turned towards town and proceeded to make an attack on the sound barrier. It was too much for me.

"You're going the wrong way, Bert," I told him.

"How do you make that out?" he said between chattering teeth.

"There's two ways to this caravan, up the towing-path or along the main road to the next turning. You've missed both."

"I'm amazed at you, Peeper. Why should I want to go anywhere near a caravan? We're going to Mortley Police

Station to check in our information with the top brass. I'm not allowed to play about on my own. I can't go swanning off and poking my nose into somebody else's murder case."

13

BUT long before we got to town, Boggis had second thoughts.

I kept working away at him about my own position, telling him how I was spending too much of my time at police stations these days, how all this publicity wasn't good for my health or my image, how people would start wagging their tongues and how there might just be another copper on duty at Mortley, who might just be linked up with Warburton and Harker in some way.

Most times it's like talking to an elephant's back leg, but this time he must have been listening. He stopped the car with a lot of tyre squeal and ended up nose-on to the pavement, front wheels actually mounted and front bumper bar all but jamming the door of the kiosk. "I want you to see this through with me, Peeper," he said. "You're something of a specialist adviser. I've a feeling things are due to burst wide open any minute, and if a snag crops up — something we need to ask you about — I want you right here where I can reach you. But I'm a reasonable man. If you're shit scared of showing your face we'll stay clear of the nick. I'll brief Len Atkinson as much as I can and we'll take it from there."

It was a longish telephone call. I watched his lips moving as he gripped the handset between ear and shoulder and played the slot like a fruit machine. Then he came out, climbed into the car and we waited some more. Atkinson turned up in his own car and after grumbling a bit about Bert's parking habits he climbed into the Consul for a confab.

"I'm getting cheesed off with you, Sergeant," he said. "I've heard all about inter-Force rivalry, but this is ridiculous. The way you're going, I shan't have any reliable officers left."

"You know Dinsdale?"

"I know him all right. He's one of the uniform blokes."

"How does he fit in, dutywise?"

"He's been on nights all this week."

"Any chance he's a mate of Warburton?"

"There's every chance, Bert, in the sense that he's a bobby working from the same station. Whether it goes any deeper than that, I can't say. There's been no reason so far to think he's bent, but neither was there about Warburton, and we know how he turned out, so you never can tell."

"What was Dinsdale doing on the night of the murder?"

"I told you, nights. He started the night shift at ten."

"So he was on duty when the bubble burst?"

"More than that. He was a member of the team that went down to the factory. I briefed him myself along with the rest. And after that he was on the team that turned over Warburton's house."

"There's coincidence for you. So if there was anything going between him and Warburton, he had a grandstand view of the débâcle. He'd have to watch his own hopes running down the sink. I suppose he must have been wearing his uniform at that time?"

"Yes. Fully kitted out. Tall hat and the lot. He'd been on foot patrol for more than two hours. He was pulled off the beat to go down with me to the factory."

"Damn. So that puts him in the clear."

"Not a bit of it, Bert. Not if you're thinking the same way I am. Before we called Dinsdale in, he was working discretionary, and on the right side of town. He had no fixed meeting points. All he had to do was prowl. So he could easily have arranged to pick up a civvy jacket somewhere, with a nylon stocking in the pocket. He wouldn't be the first beat man to go off doing his own thing."

"I wonder if that's what he did? I wonder if he was with Warburton and Harker? If he was at the factory twice, that night."

"This is pure supposition, but for the sake of argument I don't see why not. He was on trust, as all our beat bobbies must be, and he wouldn't have been missed for an hour. Even if Control had buzzed him and he hadn't answered, nobody would have thought much about it, because our town's no different from yours. There are all sorts of radio black spots where a Control message can't be picked up. Ask any Station Duty Officer. He'll tell you one of his commonest problems is not being able to reach a beat man. All they do is wait a while, then try again."

"If that was the way of it, it would be cheeky. Dinsdale meets the others at a prearranged place. He nips into Conway's van, takes his tunic off and slips on jacket and mask. Then, when they've pulled the job, he changes back to uniform and goes on pounding the pavements as though nothing had happened, knowing damned well that as soon as he collects his share he can think about chucking his job in the Force. I wonder if Dinsdale did go off the air about the right time?"

"That can only be checked by talking to the radio operator at Control. He might have logged a failure, and then again he might not. They tend not to, because they think nothing of it. But the point is, Bert, I haven't asked. I didn't want to put any hares up. Hell, it's getting so I don't know who I can trust."

"If Dinsdale was on nights last night, he'd finish at six this morning. He'd more than likely go to bed then, and he'd be up again for breakfast around midday. It's five-thirty now, so we don't know where the hell he's at."

"Oh but we do. The minute I'd heard from you, I took steps to make very sure where he was."

"Where is he?"

"Down at the police station, sitting in the canteen with two other bobbies. I sent a car straight round and had him brought in for special duty — to pick up two prisoners from Wakefield Prison and escort them back to Mortley. Only there isn't an escort job, except in my mind. You see, Bert, I can be just as devious as they can. We don't have to worry about Dinsdale. He's out of our hair, and he'll be there waiting for us the minute we need him."

"And you reckon it's worth a chance to have a look at this caravan of his?"

"I wouldn't miss it for anything, Bert. I'm here to get the facts before I lay on a snatch party."

* * *

This was the first time I'd ever seen a policeman carrying a gun. I'd seen it on telly and I knew it went on, but this bloke was sitting right alongside me in the back seat of a Police Range Rover. He was a young detective in a flak jacket, and either he was unusually stout around the middle or he had some specialized protection under there. Boggis was in front, along side the driver, having abandoned his rusty old Consul as unsuitable for the task in hand. We were driving quite slowly and I could see Bert was itching to grab the wheel and trample on the gas.

We were going slowly for a reason. As far as the caravan raid went, Boggis had been relieved of his command and was playing second fiddle to Atkinson. Atkinson and some other officers had gone the long way round in two other cars, to come on the caravan from the far side, and Boggis had been told to follow up more slowly, via the canal towing-path. I was there when Atkinson gave him his instructions and I wondered if Boggis would rebel, but he didn't seem to mind at all, except he'd rather have gone faster.

Nobody was saying much at all. Boggis mumbled the odd instruction to the driver and I offered the gun-man a cigar — which he didn't take — but otherwise we rolled on in silence.

At the canal bridge, the copper driving the Range Rover stopped and seemed a bit reluctant to start again, but after Boggis swore at him he bounced down the ramp looking thoroughly out of sorts. Once he'd straightened out on the towing-path I could see there was plenty of room. Well, maybe not plenty, but enough to let you feel you had solid ground under your wheels. There was nothing at all to see: if you didn't count the rubbish floating in the canal, a rat swimming for its life and a pair of swans that looked very snootily at us as we drove past.

The quarry Peacock had mentioned was somewhere up ahead and the caravan a bit beyond that, but the canal swung away to the right and we wouldn't have a view of either till we rounded that bend. I was a bit sorry for Bert and inclined to share his view. Atkinson and the others would be in the thick of things by now, and by the time we got there the fun would be over — if there was going to be any fun.

As things turned out, we never made it fully round that bend. We were just a few yards into the curve when Warburton and Harker appeared, dead ahead of us, going in the opposite direction.

That's who it was, and I knew it straight away, but all I could see at first was two robot figures on motor bikes, heads down, screaming towards us and closing the gap fast.

The poor old bobby at the wheel didn't know what to do, and I suppose he took the only course he could take. He braked and stopped — and we all sat there, watching it happen.

Warburton and Harker had seen the Range Rover by now, and it was funny — in a sickening way — to see what they did. I reckon their first idea was to make a 'U' turn and head back the other way. I don't know whether they could talk to each other or not, but they seemed to do all the same things. They slowed down, turned inwards, went into a wobble and nearly came off. Then, working as one man, they changed their minds, straightened up and came plunging right at us.

"The bastards are going to hit us," Boggis said, ducking down under the dashboard, and I must say that's the way it looked to me. But I kept my head half up — too spellbound to look away — and I waited to see them pile straight into us, head on.

It didn't happen that way. Twenty yards ahead of the stationary Range Rover they parted like a crocodile's jaws, and in a second they were alongside. They must have had a better view than I had, but I still didn't think they were going to make it — and they didn't make it. The bike on our left scraped along the side of the Range Rover, tilted and plunged into the canal, throwing up clouds of spray and steam. I don't know whether the other bike hit us or not, but it hit something. There was a hell of a bang, right alongside my earhole, and he disappeared.

I sat tight, feeling it was none of my business, and the three coppers set about earning themselves a medal. Boggis climbed out and leapt into the water — I'd never have believed it, but he did — and the driver went in with him. The bloke with the gun went the other way. He came back first, and stood by the Range Rover shaking his head, while Boggis and the driver clambered up the bank, dripping wet through, dragging one of the motor bike men between them.

That one was Harker. He was unconscious but not badly hurt. Warburton, it transpired, was twenty yards away, head down in a field, with a broken neck. They can mend broken necks sometimes, but not the sort Warburton had collected. His other injuries, so they told me, were of no great consequence.

I thought it was time to get out and gawp at the mess. I watched them unmask Harker and prop him up against the side of the Range Rover. I also heard the news about Warburton, but I didn't feel like going to have a look. It was quite enough for me to see his motor bike. It was half buried in a stone wall, and shorter by a foot than a motor bike should be.

"We'll need to get that bike out," Boggis said, looking not at the wall but down in the murky water. "I've got a special interest in that bike."

I slid up to him and whispered in his ear.

"Not that one, Bert. We want the other."

"Come off it, Peeper. Warburton was riding the other."

"Maybe he was. But it's Harker's bike."

★ ★ ★

283

You might say, in a way, that I was in at the kill, but I still missed out on most of the fun. They found the silver in Dinsdale's caravan and toted it back to Mortley in sacks. Sacks of silver. Just to think of it makes your knees wobble.

There was no shooting — there couldn't have been, because the gun was with Harker. And by the time they'd hauled him out of the cut he was past caring about guns.

14

SOME days later, when all the kerfuffle had died down, I had a chance to have a chat with Bert.

"It wasn't Harker who tried to run you down. It was Warburton, riding Harker's bike."

"You amaze me, Bert," I said. "When I suggested that to you, a couple of days ago, you said we'd never be able to prove it, one way or the other."

"That was before I talked to Harker. You'd be surprised how these tough little rascals can cave in sometimes. It must have been all the stress and strain of hearing about Warburton."

"So Harker admitted it wasn't him. You mean he denied it. Good God, Bert. Don't these buggers always deny it?"

"That's not the way it came out.

Harker's singing like an Italian soprano. He's admitted every job we've got against him and a dozen more besides. He's even going to plead guilty to murder if his solicitor can't talk him out of it. It was Harker who shot the two watchmen, and he's absolutely straight up about it. So you can rest easy, Peeper. When a man cleans the slate like Harker has, you can tell he's giving you a true bill."

"You asked him and he told you."

"No. I didn't mention it at all. Harker made a long statement to Detective Inspector Atkinson, and he included what Warburton had told him about the little job in Thorne Street. So I'm here to take your official complaint. It won't do you the slightest good, because we can't charge Warburton, but I can put it in and write it off. That'll keep my books straight."

"I seem to remember you said they were both guilty, in law."

"That was a technicality. Now I don't think so. And I'll tell you something else that might be helpful. Harker doesn't know *why* Warburton had a go at you. Warburton just said he had an old score to settle and he didn't say what. On top of that, if we can believe Harker, and I feel sure we can, he doesn't know much about you at all. He doesn't know you were working with Warburton and he doesn't know you work with me."

"I find that hard to believe, Bert."

"So did I, at first. But having talked to Harker I've changed my mind. I pumped him very carefully. I didn't mention you at all, directly, and neither did he. He's more in the dark than I expected him to be, and I think I know why."

"You'd better tell me then."

"Training. Habit. Natural cunning. Warburton was in the C.I.D. It was second nature to him to use informants, *but not to discuss them with people he worked with*. That's my policy too, as you very well know. I don't tell my colleagues about you."

"You told Atkinson. You told Warburton."

"Not the first time. They might have guessed, but I didn't tell them. The second time was different, because by then you'd blown yourself, in a manner of speaking, and I couldn't play it any other way. But even at that, Atkinson's from a foreign Force, and so is — was — Warburton."

I'd been worried about this aspect, and to a degree Bert's story heartened me. But I knew it was only a straw to clutch at.

"I don't see that it matters, Bert. The word's bound to get around as soon as I step into that witness box."

"What witness box? You're out of date, Peeper. We don't need you."

"What about the statement I made?"

"Atkinson's promised to hand it back to me when the case is over. I shall tear it up. We have enough evidence without it."

"From Harker, you mean?"

"From Harker, from Dinsdale and

288

from Conway. Dinsdale had no guts at all. He collapsed as soon as we started. He was in it all the way, but only for the profit. He tells me he nearly fainted when Harker started blasting off at the security staff. That had never been part of the plan, he says. Harker just went into a panic and lost control. Dinsdale will still face a murder rap, but when he makes his confession of everything else to the jury, he may very well be acquitted of murder."

"And Conway."

"Conway's a prize fool. He's still saying it wasn't him, but he's made about four separate statements, all different, and they're going to hang him, especially when the Court hears from Harker and Dinsdale about what Conway did. So you can breathe easy, Peeper. We can safely say there'll be no need to mention you at all."

"In that case, Bert," I said, "how do I stand with the silver? There was a hell of a lot — and I did tip you off about it."

"You're a mercenary little bastard, Peeper," he said, his face twitching like mad. "But I'll do my best."

* * *

And so it was that I collected a loose pile of crinkly money a few weeks later. In a way, I'd drawn twice over for some of that silver. The first pay-out had been very nice, but the second was infinitely more substantial.

I haven't made my mind up, yet, what I'm going to do with all this loot. Maybe I'll take Doreen on a continental holiday — or Stella — or maybe both. Hell, no. Not both. If I did, they'd find out about each other. And that would never do.

THE END

A GENTEEL LITTLE MURDER
Philip Daniels

Gilbert had a long-cherished plan to murder his wife. When the polished Edward entered the scene Gilbert's attitude was suddenly changed.

DEATH AT THE WEDDING
Madelaine Duke

Dr. Norah North's search for a killer takes her from a wedding to a private hospital.

MURDER FIRST CLASS
Ron Ellis

Will Detective Chief Inspector Glass find the Post Office robbers before the Executioner gets to them?

STORM CENTRE
Douglas Clark

Detective Chief Superintendent Masters, temporarily lecturing in a police staff college, finds there's more to the job than a few weeks relaxation in a rural setting.

THE MANUSCRIPT MURDERS
Roy Harley Lewis

Antiquarian bookseller Matthew Coll, acquires a rare 16th century manuscript. But when the Dutch professor who had discovered the journal is murdered, Coll begins to doubt its authenticity.

SHARENDEL
Margaret Carr

Ruth didn't want all that money. And she didn't want Aunt Cass to die. But at Sharendel things looked different. She began to wonder if she had a split personality.

THE DEATH OF ABBE DIDIER
Richard Grayson

Inspector Gautier of the Sûreté investigates three crimes which are strangely connected.

NIGHTMARE TIME
Hugh Pentecost

Have the missing major and his wife met with foul play somewhere in the Beaumont Hotel, or is their disappearance a carefully planned step in an act of treason?

BLOOD WILL OUT
Margaret Carr

Why was the manor house so oddly familiar to Elinor Howard? Who would have guessed that a Sunday School outing could lead to murder?

A FOOT IN THE GRAVE
Bruce Marshall

About to be imprisoned and tortured in Buenos Aires, John Smith escapes, only to become involved in an aeroplane hijacking.

DEAD TROUBLE
Martin Carroll

Trespassing brought Jennifer Denning more than she bargained for. She was totally unprepared for the violence which was to lie in her path.

HOURS TO KILL
Ursula Curtiss

Margaret went to New Mexico to look after her sick sister's rented house and felt a sharp edge of fear when the absent landlady arrived.

MUD IN HIS EYE
Gerald Hammond

The harbourmaster's body is found mangled beneath Major Smyle's yacht. What is the sinister significance of the illicit oysters?

THE SCAVENGERS
Bill Knox

Among the masses of struggling fish in the *Tecta*'s nets was a larger, darker, ominously motionless form . . . the body of a skin diver.

DEATH IN ARCADY
Stella Phillips

Detective Inspector Matthew Furnival works unofficially with the local police when a brutal murder takes place in a caravan camp.

THE MONTMARTRE MURDERS
Richard Grayson

Inspector Gautier of Sûreté investigates the disappearance of artist Théo, the heir to a fortune.

GRIZZLY TRAIL
Gwen Moffat

Miss Pink, alone in the Rockies, helps in a search for missing hikers, solves two cruel murders and has the most terrifying experience of her life when she meets a grizzly bear!

BLINDMAN'S BLUFF
Margaret Carr

Kate Deverill had considered suicide. It was one way out — and preferable to being murdered.

THE DRACULA MURDERS
Philip Daniels

The Horror Ball was interrupted by a spectral figure who warned the merrymakers they were tampering with the unknown.

THE LADIES
OF LAMBTON GREEN
Liza Shepherd

Why did murdered Robin Colquhoun's picture pose such a threat to the ladies of Lambton Green?

CARNABY
AND THE GAOLBREAKERS
Peter N. Walker

Detective Sergeant James Aloysius Carnaby-King is sent to prison as bait. When he joins in an escape he is thrown headfirst into a vicious murder hunt.

MURDER TO BURN
Laurie Mantell

Sergeants Steven Arrow and Lance Brendon, of the New Zealand police force, come upon a woman's body in the water. When the dead woman is identified they begin to realise that they are investigating a complex fraud.

YOU CAN HELP ME
Maisie Birmingham

Whilst running the Citizens' Advice Bureau, Kate Weatherley is attacked with no apparent motive. Then the body of one of her clients is found in her room.

DAGGERS DRAWN
Margaret Carr

Stacey Manston was the kind of girl who could take most things in her stride, but three murders were something different . . .